You're About to Become a

Privileged Woman.

INTRODUCING
PAGES & PRIVILEGES™.

It's our way of thanking you for buying
our books at your favorite retail store.

GET ALL THIS FREE

WITH JUST ONE PROOF OF PURCHASE:

◆ Hotel Discounts up to 60% at home and abroad

◆ Travel Service - Guaranteed lowest published
airfares plus 5% cash back on tickets

◆ $25 Travel Voucher

◆ Sensuous Petite Parfumerie collection ($50 value)

◆ Insider Tips Letter with sneak previews of
upcoming books

◆ Mystery Gift (if you enroll before 6/15/95)

You'll get a FREE personal card, too.
It's your passport to all these benefits– and to
even more great gifts & benefits to come!

There's no club to join. No purchase commitment. No obligation.

As a *Privileged Woman,*
you'll be entitled to all these *Free Benefits.* And *Free Gifts,* too.

To thank you for buying our books, we've designed an exclusive FREE program called *PAGES & PRIVILEGES™*. You can enroll with just one Proof of Purchase, and get the kind of luxuries that, until now, you could only read about.

Big HOTEL DISCOUNTS

A privileged woman stays in the finest hotels. And so can you—at up to 60% off! Imagine standing in a hotel check-in line and watching as the guest in front of you pays $150 for the same room that's only costing you $60. Your *Pages & Privileges* discounts are good at Sheraton, Marriott, Best Western, Hyatt and thousands of other fine hotels all over the U.S., Canada and Europe.

Free DISCOUNT TRAVEL SERVICE

A privileged woman is always jetting to romantic places. When <u>you</u> fly, just make one phone call for the lowest published airfare at time of booking—<u>or double the difference back</u>! PLUS—

you'll get a $25 voucher to use the first time you book a flight AND <u>5% cash back on every ticket you buy thereafter through the travel service</u>!

Faster than a finger snap, total chaos turned to total quiet.

Josh leaned in the doorway. Bruiser was helpfully waving smoke out the window. Calvin slowly climbed down from the table. Streaks of spaghetti sauce decorated the floor, the ceiling, the walls....

Killer recovered first. She was still standing on a chair, one arm wrapped around an obviously well-loved and well-worn stuffed animal. Her tearstained face abruptly wreathed in a smile.

"Hi, Ariel," she said.

"Hi, Ariel," Bruiser echoed.

Josh closed his eyes and clawed a hand through his hair. "Hi, Ariel," he said, his tone dryer than the Sahara. "Welcome to dinner at the Penoyer house."

Dear Reader,

Welcome to Silhouette Desire! This month, we have something special in store for you—book #1 of the *new* Silhouette miniseries, ALWAYS A BRIDESMAID! In ALWAYS A BRIDESMAID! you'll get to read how five women get the men of their dreams. Each book will be featured in a different Silhouette series…one book a month beginning this month with *The Engagement Party* by Barbara Boswell.

In addition, we've got a wonderful MAN OF THE MONTH by award-winning author Jennifer Greene called *Single Dad*. Josh is a hero you'll never forget.

Don't miss *Dr. Daddy*, book #3 in Elizabeth Bevarly's series FROM HERE TO MATERNITY. And a new series, WEDDING BELLES, by Carole Buck launches with the charming *Annie Says I Do*.

A book by Jackie Merritt is always a treat, and she's sure to win new fans—and please her present admirers—with *Hesitant Husband*. And Anne Marie Winston's *Rancher's Wife* completes what I feel is a perfect month!

Silhouette Desire—you've just got to read them all!

Enjoy!

Lucia Macro
Senior Editor

Please address questions and book requests to:
Silhouette Reader Service
U.S.: 3010 Walden Ave., P.O. Box 1325, Buffalo, NY 14269
Canadian: P.O. Box 609, Fort Erie, Ont. L2A 5X3

JENNIFER GREENE
SINGLE DAD

SILHOUETTE *Desire*®

™ Published by Silhouette Books

America's Publisher of Contemporary Romance

If you purchased this book without a cover you should be aware that this book is stolen property. It was reported as "unsold and destroyed" to the publisher, and neither the author nor the publisher has received any payment for this "stripped book."

 SILHOUETTE BOOKS

ISBN 0-373-05931-0

SINGLE DAD

Copyright © 1995 by Jennifer Greene

All rights reserved. Except for use in any review, the reproduction or utilization of this work in whole or in part in any form by any electronic, mechanical or other means, now known or hereafter invented, including xerography, photocopying and recording, or in any information storage or retrieval system, is forbidden without the written permission of the editorial office, Silhouette Books, 300 East 42nd Street, New York, NY 10017 U.S.A.

All characters in this book have no existence outside the imagination of the author and have no relation whatsoever to anyone bearing the same name or names. They are not even distantly inspired by any individual known or unknown to the author, and all incidents are pure invention.

This edition published by arrangement with Harlequin Enterprises B.V.

® and TM are trademarks of Harlequin Enterprises B.V., used under license. Trademarks indicated with ® are registered in the United States Patent and Trademark Office, the Canadian Trade Marks Office and in other countries.

Printed in U.S.A.

JENNIFER GREENE

lives near Lake Michigan with her husband and two children. Before writing full-time, she worked as a teacher and personnel manager. Michigan State University honored her as an "outstanding woman graduate" for her work with women on campus.

Ms. Greene has written more than forty category romances, for which she has won numerous awards, including the RITA for Best Short Contemporary Book, and both a Best Series Author and a Lifetime Achievement award from *Romantic Times*.

Printed in U.S.A.

One

"**W**ell, of course you're shook up that this guy asked you to dinner, Jeanne. You spend all day with serial killers and werewolves. You haven't been off that computer in so long that you've probably forgotten what a real, normal human male looks like...."

The shop bell tinkled. Hugging the telephone receiver to her cheek, Ariel Lindstrom glanced through the doorway of the back room, but she didn't see any customers.

"...An invitation to dinner doesn't mean you have to marry him, for Pete's sake. Just go out and have fun. What's so hard?...of *course* you don't have anything to wear. You haven't been shopping since the turn of the decade. Come on over. I'll find you something in my closet...so my taste is a little wild. It wouldn't kill you to break out a little...."

Ariel was on a roll—giving advice was so much fun—but her gaze still searched the main room of the shop. *Someone* must have come in. The bell only rang when the door opened—yet there wasn't a soul in sight. The afternoon had turned blistering, broiling, butter-burn hot—unreasonably hot, even for a Connecticut July summer day. Everyone in Woodridge had holed up behind their air conditioners or fans. Her partner, Dot, had the day off and the shop had been as quiet as a tomb since lunch.

"...So what if he gets the wrong idea? I hope he does. When's the last time you were kissed? The Civil War? It's about that long since you pried yourself away from that book you've been working on...."

Ariel rose on tiptoe and craned her neck, but nothing seemed to be stirring in the shop. When the phone first rang, she'd been soldering the sterling clasp on a 1914 lavaliere. Old jewelry was the specialty of the gift store; the first two aisles of the shop were packed with nests of baubles displayed on velvet. The stock also ran to the gaudy, bright and whimsical. Crystal dragons and unicorns had a special niche in a sunlit corner. Stained glass doodads shot prisms of rainbow colors from another nook. Beyond the door, she'd set up a "magic corner" for kids, with crystal balls and wands and magic tricks.

There. Ariel's gaze narrowed. She couldn't see the body from this angle, but peeking out from the edge of the magic aisle was the tip of a tennis shoe. A laceless, orange fluorescent tennis shoe—distinctly a child-size. She almost chuckled aloud. "I'm not through with you, Jeanne, so don't think you're off the hook. But I'll have to call you back. I have a customer."

Her friend sounded enormously relieved to escape the conversation. Ariel hung up the receiver and headed straight for the telltale shoe.

The entire world knew she was a sucker for kids, but this one was a true heart stealer. The child raised huge, stricken, guilty eyes the instant she spotted Ariel. The urchin was maybe five. A girl, dressed in a Red Sox T-shirt and stringy cutoffs, with two straggly brunette pigtails jammed under a backward baseball cap. Her nose had a smudge. Both knees had healing scrapes. Her face was downright plain—except for those liquid chocolate eyes—but lack of cuteness certainly hadn't affected her self-confidence. Her whole belligerent posture spoke of smart-aleck bravado.

It wasn't hard for Ariel to relate. She'd never been short of attitude herself at that age. Ariel crouched down by the child. "Hi there. What's your name?"

"Killer."

"Killer, huh? Well, if that isn't a great name, I don't know what is. Are you shopping for anything special today?"

Those skinny shoulders pulled off a huge shrug. "I just wanted to look at stuff. Like the magic tricks and things like that. I wasn't gonna take anything—"

"Hey, I never thought you were. It's a great afternoon to mess with magic. I'll show you a couple of tricks if you want. Too hot to be playing outside, isn't it?" Ariel tacked on casually, "Where's your mom, sweetie?"

The question was never meant to be complicated. The neighborhood kids often made Treasures into a pit stop on a lazy afternoon. It was a middle-class suburb; lots of moms worked, and the hillside shop was within easy walking distance from the schools.

Ariel only asked about the missing mom because she wanted to make sure the little one had permission to be here. She never expected the child to take the question so literally.

"My mom split. She took off because she didn't want us kids anymore. We all made too many messes and drove her crazy."

The child's tone was matter-of-fact, no bid for sympathy, yet Ariel felt an instant, violent tug of kinship. Divorces were so every-day common that another broken-home story was hardly headline news, but growing up, she'd had ample experience being shrapnel in the divorce wars. At twenty-nine, she had no faith in the institution of marriage and even less belief in "forevers." Still she hated to see a mite-size urchin stuck learning those painful lessons so young.

And could the mite talk. Eek. Once the urchin began chattering, she barely stopped for breath.

Her real name was Patrice, but no one called her anything but Killer. Her last name was Penoyer. Her great-grandfather was Hungarian, but he'd been dead for just about forever. She was six. Her dad couldn't braid hair worth squat. Her two older brothers couldn't play any girl games. She was supposed to start first grade in the fall, but her brothers had filled her in about the boring school business. She wasn't interested and she wasn't going. Ever. Her best friend was Boober. Boober was nine feet tall and liked magic, which was a secret she was keeping from her dad. "Because my dad doesn't believe in magic. At *all*."

"He doesn't, hmm?" By then, Ariel had shown her the disappearing scarf trick and miraculously made a fifty-cent piece appear from behind the child's left ear. She didn't mind ignoring work and entertaining the little one. Give or take the unknown gender of the imaginary friend "Boober," there didn't seem to be any females in the child's life, and she was clearly lonesome for some company. Only the clock over the antique cash register kept ticking, and the child showed no signs of winding down or leaving.

"Honey, are you sure it's okay that you're still here? No one's expecting you at home, are they?"

Those liquid chocolate eyes turned stricken again. "Uh-oh. Can you read me the time?"

"It's just after four o'clock," Ariel told her.

"Oh, cripes. Oh, double cripes. I gotta *go!*

That was it. The child galloped for the door; the bell tinkled, and then she was gone, rounding the corner of the building down the alley and out of sight.

Ariel rubbed the back of her neck, amused and bemused by the whole encounter. It wasn't hard to understand why she felt such a fast, fierce emotional bond with the gregarious little smart aleck. The child reminded her of herself at that age, but it would be silly to take the bond too seriously. Who knew if she'd ever see the urchin again?

And playtime was over. She'd brilliantly managed to avoid doing a lick of work all afternoon—no guilt there; she'd never been plagued by either ambition or practicality—but bills refused to disappear by osmosis. She pivoted on her heel and started walking toward the back room...when she suddenly noticed the missing unicorn.

The crystal unicorns had become a favorite with collectors. Because each tiny figure was unique, Ariel had decided to display each piece on its own tiny mirror. The mirror with nothing on it stood out like a beacon.

No one had been in the shop but Killer, and the price tag for the missing unicorn was forty-five bucks. A little late, Ariel recalled finding the child at the corner between the magic aisle and the crystal display—and the stricken, guilty look in those chocolate eyes.

Damn.

For a short five seconds, Ariel debated tracking down her miniature thief. The little delinquent had mentioned her last name. Penoyer? Wasn't that it? Nothing so common that scouting a telephone number should be too challenging—if she wanted her unicorn or her forty-five bucks back.

The mental debate didn't last long. The money was no big deal; the principle mattered more, but the redline truth was that she'd rather chew rats than get the child in trouble. The image of that dad who didn't believe in magic—"at *all*"— prowled through her mind.

Killer's dad sounded like a hard-core realist. Stern. Unbending. An unyielding rule lover. Basing her judgment on the few comments the child had made about him was hardly fair, but it didn't really matter if she was right or wrong. She'd never know him. One lost unicorn simply wasn't worth the risk of getting the child in trouble, and that was that.

"Ariel!"

"Hmm." Ariel heard her partner calling, but she didn't look up from the workbench. The chances of Dot actually needing her for anything were about five million to one. It was nearly seven—closing time— which Dot could handle blindfolded in her sleep.

Spread in front of Ariel was a tray of seed pearls. She adjusted the gooseneck lamp for the third time.

The coral cameo brooch was a real find. A little cracked, but not too bad. The brooch was circled with seed pearls, a style common around 1910, but two pearls had been missing when the piece came in. Fixing it was no challenge, but finding two seed pearls of the right color and size was a real blinger.

"Ariel! There's someone out here to see you!"

"Hmm." Using tweezers and a magnifying glass, she held up another seed pearl to the light. Dot had been handling customers for several hours, the same amount of time she'd buried herself in the back with repair projects. She was determined to finish this last one before calling it quits.

The two-day heat spell hadn't broken, and the air-conditioning just refused to reach back here. She'd jettisoned her shoes hours ago, piled and pinned her long blond hair off her neck, hiked up her skirt and unbuttoned her blouse. She was still hot. And beginning to suffer from starvation.

She studied another seed pearl in the lamplight, but her mind was indulging in a lustful, dawdling daydream about bathtubs and butter-brickle ice cream. The daydream wasn't as good as a nice, wicked fantasy about sex—but almost. Her apartment was over the shop. If she ever finished this blasted brooch, she just might climb the stairs, lock the door, strip and immerse herself in a cool scented bath, a spoon and a pint of ice cream in hand. So it was a little decadent. Who'd know? Who'd care?

And she could already taste that to-die-for-delicious butter brickle.

"Ariel, for heaven's sakes, didn't you hear me calling you?"

"Hmm? Oh. Sorry, Dot, my mind was in another universe...." She spun around, expecting to see her partner in the doorway—which she did. But Dorothy, with her short-cropped Afro and bifocals and tastefully tailored clothes, had always been the stable member of their pair. Why she was standing there, winking and rolling her eyes, was beyond Ariel. "What's wrong?"

"Nothing." Dot shot her another "meaningful" wink. "I just wanted to tell you that I'm leaving. The register's locked and the Closed sign is up, so you won't be disturbed. I'll be in tomorrow at nine."

"Fine, see you tomorrow." Ariel still hadn't fathomed what all the winking was about, until her six-foot friend shifted past the doorway.

There were two people just behind Dot. A man and a child. Ariel recognized the miniature female delinquent in the orange fluorescent tennies in a heart's blink—she'd thought about Killer more than once over the past two days. But it was Killer's dad who riveted her attention.

She didn't have to guess about the family connection—the physical resemblance was unmistakable. Mr. Penoyer had the same shock of thick unruly hair, midnight black, and the same liquid dark eyes as his daughter. But the squirt must have inherited her homely bones from some other source, because her daddy was one hell of a looker.

Ariel's complete distrust in the institution of marriage never meant she was antimen. It had been a while, though, since she met a lightning bolt who inspired her feminine hormones to a 911 red-alert status. He wasn't huge, maybe five feet ten, but the package was all lean, wired muscle. Apparently he'd come straight here after a day of working in the heat, because he carried a hard hat in one hand, and he was dressed in jeans, a worn navy T-shirt and scuffed work boots.

Judging from the character lines etched around his eyes, he was in his mid-thirties. Judging from the scowl cut deep as a well on his forehead, he was smoking with tension and temper. It wasn't hard to figure out that he didn't want to be here. The phrase "volatile powder keg" shot through her mind, followed by the disgracefully wayward thought that he'd be an incredible handful in bed—dangerous and exciting and unpredictable.

Not that his skills as a lover were relevant to anything. She wasn't prospecting. It was just an objective observation.

In those same few seconds, he seemed to make some instantaneous objective observations about her, too. Those dark eyes laddered up her bare feet to her hiked-up skirt to her open-collared shirt to her wildly disarrayed blond hair. Modesty hadn't been her concern in the privacy of the back room. Actually, modesty was rarely a front-line priority with her anyway—good grief, a body was a body. But *hers* suddenly felt different, alive and aware and definitely exposed. Heaven knew what he'd expected, but his gaze reflected the same kind of wariness he'd show an open vial of nitro.

"You're the owner of this place? Ariel Lindstrom?"

He sounded so doubtful that she was tempted to offer him ID. "Yes."

"Well, I'm Josh Penoyer. Patrice's father." With two firm hands on her shoulders, Killer was ousted from the safe hiding place behind his legs. "My daughter has something to say to you." Killer clearly wasn't fond of this plan, because she burrowed straight back for her daddy's arms. "Patrice." There was no meanness to his tone, but it wasn't hard to identify the immobility of rock. Dad wasn't gonna budge. The little one lifted dread-filled eyes. Sotto voce, he prompted her, "We're sorry...."

"We're sorry. *Very* sorry we took your unicorn." Said-offending unicorn came out of a shorts pocket, wrapped protectively in several miles of tissue, and was placed on Ariel's workbench.

"Oh, sweetheart..." Ariel started to say, but she was cut off.

"We have a little more to say than that, don't we, Patrice?"

"Yeah." Killer had to take a huge breath before she could get out the rest of the prepared speech. "We unnerstand that you could call the cops and put me away for the rest of my life, but we're hoping you won't. Because I would never steal anything again as long as I live. And because I'm real sorry. And because you were nice, and that makes it extra bad that I stole something from you, and I'll probably never be able to forgive myself, even in my whole life."

Ariel couldn't wait another second before pushing off the stool and crouching down to the child's level. "Well, we certainly can't have you feeling *that* bad. It takes a big person to own up to her mistakes, Killer, and it means a lot to me that you did that. You brought the unicorn back, and you apologized. That squares things with me just fine."

She raised her eyes to Killer's dad. "Really. The whole thing's forgotten as far as I'm concerned, Mr. Penoyer."

"Josh," he corrected her, which was about the last word he said. His parental mission accomplished, he scooped up his daughter and gave her a riding seat on the back of his shoulders—where the little one was prevented from touching anything else in the shop, Ariel noted humorously. Less than a minute later, the two exited the store in a tinkle of bells.

From the window, Ariel watched him strap Killer into a dusty red Bronco, then take off. As hot and tired as she was, she stood there for a few more minutes. Belatedly she recognized that Josh had looked exhausted and hot, too, but that hadn't stopped him from making his child's problem a priority. That said a lot about his values as a dad. It said even more about him as a man.

She'd pegged him as a hard-core realist—positively her opposite in temperament—but Ariel had no problem admitting that she'd been charmed. Seriously and sincerely charmed. Killer's behavior with her dad had been as revealing as a blueprint. Even when Josh had looked intimidatingly ready to blow the lid off that temper, the urchin had burrowed straight for his arms. He might get mad, but no way was his daughter afraid of him. The strong, loving bond between the two had been rich and rare, a measure of the man and his ability to love. Ariel hadn't met a special man like that in a long time.

She abruptly turned around and headed for the back stairs. It was tempting to mull and muse all night about Josh—but far more sensible to force her mind back on butter-brickle. Her stomach was growling—a problem she could easily fix. And she'd learned young to steer clear of problems that she couldn't. The chances of her seeing either of the Penoyers again seemed doubtful. It was best to forget them.

"She was pretty, wasn't she, Dad? Didn't you think she was pretty?"

Since it was the fourth time Killer had asked the question during the drive home, Josh figured he wasn't going to get out of an answer. "Yeah, sure," he said flatly. Truthfully, he thought that descriptive epitaph was an awfully pale peg for Ms. Lindstrom. Sexy. Wild. Flighty. Those were more like it.

"Did you like her, Dad?"

"Sure, I liked her." He liked fireworks. He liked race cars and storms. And just because he was thirty-four and divorced didn't mean he was dead from the waist down. He liked long-legged, long-haired blondes built with a memorable upper deck just fine. But a grown man didn't have to dip his hand in flames to know there were unpleasant consequences to playing with fire.

"Wasn't she nice? Didn't you think she was nice?"

"Yeah, Ms. Lindstrom was nice. But if you think talking about her is going to distract me from what you did, you're dreaming. I'm still mad at you. What you did was real, real wrong, Patrice."

"I know."

Aw, hell. Her lower lip was starting to tremble. Dammit, he hated it when the squirt did that.

Josh jammed a hand through his hair as he turned the corner. Calvin was fourteen, Bruiser thirteen. God knew they got into all kinds of mischief, but it was *boy* trouble, the kind Josh understood. The kind of stuff his daughter got into confused him. He was just no expert at six-year-old girls, and pretending he was qualified to be both Mom and Dad was a full-time challenge.

He sneaked another peek.

The lip was still trembling.

"Look, I can't just forget it."

"I know," Killer said pitifully.

"We'll go home. Have dinner. But after that, you go straight to your room. No playing. And no TV tonight." His voice was stern, but he checked her face again. Was the punishment too mean?

"Okay." A single tear dribbled down his daughter's cheek, caught on a smudge of dirt, then drooled the rest of the way down her neck.

Josh glanced at traffic behind him, then reached over and gently wiped the tear away. "You *have* to have a punishment when you do something this serious. Could you try and understand that? It's my job as a dad, for Pete's sake. I *have* to do this, Killer."

"I said okay."

Maybe it was "okay," but he saw another tear welling. Nothing with Calvin or Bruiser had ever been this complicated. He'd never hesitated to give the boys a swat on the behind at this age—like if they'd run in the street or broken a window—and for sure, stealing rated up there as a spanking offense. But somehow he'd never managed to lay a hand on Killer. Even when he was mad enough to strangle her—and God knew, the squirt could be exasperating—he had to work like a dog to even raise his voice. Something in those big brown eyes sabotaged him every time. They made him feel like melting. They made him feel like mush. They made him feel guilty.

Josh swung into the driveway, mentally damning Nancy for taking off on him and the kids. The divorce had been final for a year now. Whatever had gone wrong in the relationship, he hadn't had time to figure out. He was too busy coping with work, bills, dishes, cooking, laundry, two teenage sons and a six-year-old daughter.

Still, as long as he ran sixty miles an hour, he'd really believed that he'd *been* coping—until a problem like this happened. "I still don't get it. What possessed you to take that unicorn thing?" he asked his daughter.

"It was pretty."

"Yeah? So? Lots of things are pretty, but if it's not yours, you don't touch it. You *know* that."

"I know, Dad."

Somehow he was failing to gain any comprehension of the six-year-old feminine mind. "Did you ever see me take anything that wasn't mine?"

"No, Daddy."

"Did you ever see me touch anything that didn't belong to me?"

"No, Daddy."

He was parked, the engine off, and she wanted out of the Bronco in the worst way. It wasn't as if he were gaining any ground. "Okay, skedaddle. I'll be in to make dinner in just a second."

She skedaddled faster than a puppy with a burr, but Josh sat in the silence for a moment longer. Their house was at the end of a cul-de-sac on the hilltop. Matching frame bungalows lined the street, typical of a working-class neighborhood. Nothing fancy, but it wasn't rough. The kids had a ravine and woods to play in. Clusters of old maples and ash and birch trees lined the block. Anyone could identify his house as being womanless, though.

Two rusty bicycles lay abandoned in the yard, not put away. The curtains in the front window didn't hang the way a woman seemed to genetically know how to hang the blasted things. There were no flowers planted in the beds. And inside, Josh already knew he was going to find dirty glasses, thrown towels, shoes and clothes that reproduced in the strangest places, and a bathroom that risked being condemned by the health department. His bedroom may—*may*—have been left sacrosanct, but for sure the only company he was likely to find in that lonely double bed was one of the boy's basketballs.

Josh sighed with exasperation. He'd screwed up plenty in his life, but he valued integrity and tried to pass on that value to his kids. The problem was, it was hard to climb all over his daughter for falling prey to an irresistible impulse...when he personally knew how easily that could happen.

He'd taken one look at Ms. Lindstrom and felt as if he'd stepped in a land mine of blatant, irresistible impulses. He'd bet the bank that silvery blond hair reached her waist in length. The green eyes and pearl skin and that soft mouth still lingered in his mind. So did the swell of her breasts peeking out of that open-throated shirt. He suddenly recalled—to the day—how long he'd been celibate, which sure as hell wasn't his nature or his choice.

It wasn't as if anything had changed. There wasn't a sane woman on the planet who'd take him and his brood on. And assuming he had the time and energy to pursue a woman—which he didn't—he'd never pick a flighty seller-of-magic. His kids needed stability.

Hell, so did he. But one look in those almond-shaped eyes had sparked a chemical combustion that woke up every masculine hormone. He likened it to trying to sleep when someone was hitting you over the head with a club.

Josh wasn't going to *do* anything about it.

He just wasn't going to lie to himself and pretend the feeling never happened. Irresistible impulses were a human frailty. Six-year-olds had an understandably difficult problem controlling them. A man his age—thank God—was smarter, older, wiser.

The safest thing to do was to put her straight, totally and completely, out of his mind.

And he did.

Two

Uh-oh. It was a good thing that Ariel glanced up when the tinkling of the bell announced someone had entered the store. A second later, and she might have missed the urchin in the backward baseball cap and oversize Pittsburgh Steelers T-shirt.

She hadn't seen Patrice in days—nor expected to—but temporarily she had her hands full. The entire morning had been an exercise in commotion and locomotion. Dot wasn't due in until three. The phone refused to stop ringing; three browsers were wandering around; a woman lunch shopper was waiting at the cash register to buy earrings; and Ariel was stuck behind the jewelry counter with a gentleman who was sweating blood, trying to pick out a present for his wife.

The young blond man fingered a moonstone-and-mother-of-pearl pendant, which was about the ninetieth thing he'd considered, and shot her a helpless look. "Do you think she'll like it?"

Since Ariel had never met his wife, she didn't have a clue. "I think it's beautiful myself, and I don't see how you can go too wrong with that—not if she likes antiquey-type jewelry."

"She loves all kinds of antiquey stuff. But this has to be special." He confided, "We've been married six months today."

By today's divorce statistics, enduring six months together was probably a record, but Ariel had no time to give him an "attaboy." The woman at the cash register was impatiently tapping her foot. The phone rang again. And normally Ariel would have been happy to spend all day with blondie—he was really a darling, just a little short in the decision-making department. But she felt uneasy about Killer being in the store alone, and the urchin had already disappeared from sight.

"I'll tell you what," she told the gentleman. "You think about this for a minute, while I take care of the lady up front, and I'll be right back." She jogged to the front, quickly dealt with the phone call, rang up the sale, bagged it, answered a fast question from the browsers on stained-glass prices and galloped back to her man.

En route, she caught a glimpse of the miniature brunette near the magic aisle, which was enough to relieve her mind.

She was delighted to see the child again. She also believed the little one's ardent promises about never stealing again. It was just that she'd met few adults who could keep their promises—especially ardently made promises—and she wasn't about to believe the six-year-old had mastered temptation. Thankfully, the magic tricks were all safely locked inside the glass cabinet. She really didn't want to see the urchin get into any more trouble.

The gentleman eventually chose a black-button pearl bracelet and paid—bless him!—in cash; the earrings shopper left; and the three browsers meandered to the front with their stained-glass window ornaments. Once they were gone, the transition from commotion to total silence was astoundingly quick. Ariel hustled toward the magic aisle.

Killer's nose was pressed to the glass. "Hi," she said, when Ariel crouched down.

"Hi, back."

"I have money today." To illustrate proof, Killer pushed up the Pittsburgh Steelers T-shirt and dug in the pockets of her cherry-red shorts. Once all the pockets were turned inside out, five dollars in crumpled ones and change gradually accumulated on the counter.

"Wow. You have lots of money."

"I want a magic trick. If that's okay." She hesitated. "I wasn't sure if it was okay if I came back. Maybe you're still mad at me."

"I was never mad at you, Killer. You made a mistake. I've made a few mistakes myself. And you're welcome to come in the store as often as you want, sweetie, as long as you have your dad's permission."

"He's gone during the day. But I asked Mary Sue. She takes care of me, and she said yes. I can pretty much go anyplace as long as I don't have to cross streets, and all I gotta do to get here is walk down the ravine and then up the sidewalk and then down the alley."

Well, that settled the issue of permission, but the purchase of the magic trick was a more complicated business. The quest for the Holy Grail never took this long. The goal was to dazzle and bedazzle her older brothers, but finding a magic trick that Killer could handle and her older brothers couldn't figure out took some experimenting.

They tried card tricks. They tried cutting-rope tricks. They made a quarter miraculously disappear in a glass of water, and a scarf miraculously change color, and a broken toothpick miraculously heal itself. By then, Killer was chattering six for a dozen. The topic strayed from magic to girl stuff. Important things, like how to braid hair. Dolls. Perfume. Best friends. How disgusting boys were—especially Tommy Bradley.

"He tried to kiss me," Killer said with a scrunch of her nose. "What a yuck."

"Tommy Bradley lacks a little technique, hmm?"

"He really gives me the creeps—don't tell my dad about that, okay? My dad wouldn't like it if a boy tried to kiss me. He already told me he's not gonna let me date until I'm forty-five. As if I'd want to."

"I won't tell," Ariel said gravely.

"I'm gonna grow my hair just like you. And wear earrings just like you. I just have to get a little older about the earrings, Dad says."

Half the little one's conversation was peppered with whatever her dad said and thought. Ariel couldn't help but picture Josh surviving the incessant stream of girl talk. She'd never rationed smiles—or laughter—and she wasn't that busy. It was easy to give the child the female companionship she was so poignantly lonesome for.

Killer had fresh French braids and the bagged-up
quarter magic trick—discounted—when she skipped
out of the store around three.

Fifteen minutes later, Ariel discovered the missing
ruby-eyed dragon.

Lightning striped the black sky. Rain slashed down
in gusty torrents. After five days of killing heat, the
storm was more than welcome, but Josh was soaked
through by the time he jogged from the Bronco
through the alley and up the back metal stairs. When
he reached the top, rain drizzled down his neck and
matted his eyelashes. Still, he hesitated before knocking.

He *really* didn't want to be here.

Killer had told him that Ariel lived over the shop,
and lights shone through the pale curtains, fair evidence that she was at home. It was past eight. He'd
been to his place, had dinner and messed around with
the kids for as long as he could procrastinate this little chore. Any later than this, and an unexpected caller
at night would probably scare a woman alone. Hell, an
unexpected guy caller could probably scare her now,
but at least eight o'clock was still reasonably early.

He just really didn't want to knock on that door.

Rain sluiced through his hair and rivered off his
denim jacket. Impatiently he set his jaw, squared his
shoulders. And firmly back-knuckled the door.

The back light popped on. He heard her, on the
other side, undoing a dead bolt and locks. His shoulder muscles were bunched and braced even before she
poked her head out.

"Josh?" Her clear-bell voice made his name sound
like a question, but there didn't seem to be any star-

tled shock in her expression. She glanced at him, chuckled as she said, "Good grief, are you *wet!* Come on in, before you drown out there—" and then looked down and past him.

It wasn't hard to guess that she was searching for another body. "Killer isn't with me. Killer is grounded for the rest of her life," he informed her.

"Ah."

The twinkle of humor in her eyes disarmed him— maybe she didn't know about his daughter's latest shoplifting escapade? Either way, he positively wanted this encounter over quick. One horrified glance had revealed that she was in pajamas. Silky, sexy, scarlet pajamas. And the last time he'd seen her, her hair had been all piled up. Now it was down, brushed smooth, about three miles of silvery-gold taffy that swished almost to her waist. He averted his eyes, trying to look nowhere, not at her place and for sure not at her, as he dug inside his jacket for the small wrapped package. "I believe this dragon thingamabog belongs to you."

"Yeah, I'm afraid it does." Her soft green eyes met his. "I realized she had it about three minutes after she left the shop."

"You know she took it? Since yesterday afternoon?"

"Yes. I just wasn't sure what to do. I really didn't want to get her into any more trouble." She hesitated. "Look, wouldn't you like to come in and dry off for a few minutes? I've got some coffee on the stove. You want a splash of brandy in it?"

"I…" He never planned on coming in, not once he realized she was dressed for bed. But the friendly offer for coffee threw him. She could have been madder than a wet hen—hell, she could have called the cops on his kid. If there was some protocol for a single dad in this situation, he just didn't know what it was. "I never meant to take up your evening. I just wanted to give the thing back to you and apologize."

"I understand...but you're worried about your daughter, aren't you? Maybe it'd help if we talked about it."

Personally, Josh never found that talking helped much of anything. But he figured he owed her some kind of explanation for his daughter's recent klepto-maniac streak, and he didn't want Ariel thinking he was the kind of dad who didn't give a damn about his kids. So gingerly he stepped inside.

She took his jacket. And he had to heel off his boots or risk tracking in mud. The next thing he knew, he had a fragile-looking china cup in his hands, filled with some kind of fancy gourmet coffee, fragrant and rich and topped off with a splash of brandy.

"Come on in the living room. More comfortable to sit in there," she said easily.

He took a gulp of the brew as he followed her, hop-ing the liquor might settle his nerves. It didn't. Guess-ing conservatively, he figured the chances of his being comfortable around her rivaled the odds of a federal balanced budget. There'd be colonies on Mars first.

"I'm crazy about your daughter, you know." She curled up in the corner of the couch, and motioned him to the closest chair. Her sweep of a smile seemed honest and warm. Somehow that smile made it easier for him to talk than he'd expected.

"She's crazy about you, too. Practically everything she's said in the last week was a quote from you. Don't take this wrong, okay? But I think half the problem is this attachment she's formed to you."

Ariel nodded thoughtfully. "I had the feeling she was really lonesome for a woman's company."

"I *know* she's lonesome for a woman's company. She took her mom's leaving hard. I have two boys...."

"She told me about her brothers."

Josh rubbed his jaw. "Nancy's leaving, the divorce, hasn't been easy on any of them. But Killer definitely had the hardest time with it. And still is. That's no excuse for stealing. She knows better. But I don't want you thinking she's a bad kid. She's not bad. She's..." Well, the squirt was damn near perfect in his eyes—always had been. Yes, exasperating and exhausting and an incredibly confusing little female person, but a light in his life like nothing else. Only, how was a grown man supposed to put that in words?

"I never thought she was bad, Josh," Ariel said gently. "In fact, I can remember shoplifting a pack of gum when I was that age."

"Shoplifting a quarter pack of gum is a little different than taking off with something that cost—what *was* that dragon thing worth, anyway?"

"Around sixty dollars. But I doubt she had any understanding of its dollar value. It looked like a little thing to her. Just something pretty. And she's of the age where she'd know about dragons from fairy tales. You know, you won't break that chair if you sit back in it," she murmured with amusement.

Josh wasn't worried about breaking the chair. He was worried about him. When she didn't immediately hustle to some back room for a robe or cover-up, it finally registered that the scarlet outfit wasn't pajamas. Apparently it was just one of those gummy-silk things that women walked around in these days. The shirtish

top was loose, oversize. Not even suggestive of bed-
rooms or bedroom attire, if a guy didn't have a dirty
mind.

Josh was trying to keep his mind clean. He was trying, in fact, to think like a celibate monk. Only, he'd
never been a monk, and a full bottle of bleach wasn't
likely to wash the X-rated thoughts racing through his
mind.

She was really something. And so was her place.

The building was a good hundred years old, he
guessed. The tall-pitched ceiling had to be hell on her
heating bills. The old-fashioned windows were draft
suckers. A white marble—cracked marble—fireplace
stood in the far corner, another drafty nightmare if it
wasn't regularly maintenanced and cared for. She
probably had to worry about blinking lights with wiring this old. Josh told himself he was judging the
whole thing from an objective masculine perspective,
but the truth was, he wasn't thinking about her fireplace flue.

The carpet was a pale water blue and as plushy as a
sponge. The couch and chairs had sink-deep cush-
ions, the fabric soft and that same muted blue color.
One lamp had a fringed shade, and the other—the one
behind her head—was Tiffany-style, with roses against
a blue sky background. Piles of candles sat on her
coffee table. Not unused candles, like in any *normal*
place, but vanilla-and spice-scented candles that she
obviously lit and enjoyed, because the wax had swirled
and pooled in the holders. She had a crystal ball on the
mantel. An honest-to-Pete crystal ball, like witches
used, and it picked up all the soft colors from everywhere and reflected them right back.

Nothing was bright. Nothing was noisy. There wasn't a football in sight, no doll carriages to trip over, no dirty dishes, no video game screeching. Every scent, texture and sound was distinctly sensual—hedonistically, worrisomely sensual—and so was she.

It wasn't her fault, Josh kept telling himself, that she looked like a guy's seductive fantasy of a dream lover. The long legs were probably genetic. Blond hair probably ran in her family, too. It wasn't as if she'd done anything to sell the package. Her hair had no special style, not full of gunky hairspray. It was just so silky, so long, that any man was naturally going to imagine his hands wrapped in it. And she was wearing a gold pendant—nothing big or gaudy, but the little chunk was trapped in the shadow of her plump breasts, drawing his eyes there. Forcing his eyes to the dip of ivory flesh in the vee of her shirt . . . especially when she was bending right over him.

"Would you like some more?"

Belatedly he realized she was holding the coffeepot, trying to offer him a refill. "Maybe one more quick one," he said, then abruptly wiped a hand over his face. He wished he hadn't said "Quick one."

"A little more brandy, too?"

"No brandy for me this time, but thanks." If that splash of brandy was responsible for this abrupt surge of hormones, he wanted no more of it. He wanted to kick himself. Maybe it had been a month of Sundays since he'd been alone with a woman, but he knew how to behave around one. He was also a practical, grounded, blue-collar kind of guy. He knew damn well when a lady was way, way out of his realm.

She poured them both more coffee, and carried her cup back to the couch, tucking her legs under her. "Killer never told me what you did for a living...."

"I'm an electrical contractor." He almost chuckled. She cocked her head, expressing interest, but he couldn't fathom a woman who was into crystal balls wanting to hear anything about wiring and electric circuits. It was past time he acted like a grown man who could handle a conversation without stuttering. "Have you owned your shop long?"

"Treasures? About four years now." She grinned. "I think you met my partner the other day... the six-foot-tall black woman with the bifocals and the gorgeous mocha skin? Her real name is Dorothy, but her nickname's always been Dot."

He remembered the Amazon. When he walked in the shop, she'd treated him like handling lost-soul construction workers was the most fun she'd had all day. "She has quite a sense of humor."

"She's wonderful. We met at an antique jewelry auction a million years ago, and clicked right away. I used to work with silver, designing pieces, but I was never good enough to make a living at it. But I know jewelry, and she knows about the business end of running a shop. When the building came up for sale about four years ago, we decided to give it a go together."

"You do okay?"

"Better than most gift stores, I suspect. The location's great, and we've kept the payroll down to just the two of us and a part-time guy. Unique jewelry is our main thing. Even in recession times, most women can't resist a new bangle or pair of earrings. Me, either. In fact, that's what I try and stock—what I can't resist," she admitted humorously. "Anyway, we're hardly banking millions, but we're keeping afloat."

"You seem to like kids...." Jeez. Talking with her wasn't coming half as hard as he'd expected, but there were clearly some subjects that made her light up like a Christmas tree. She darn near bounced with enthusiasm, her smile turned up a thousand wattage.

"I'm *crazy* about kids. Wish I had a dozen of my own, but I make do, borrowing nieces and nephews and any relatives' kids I can beg, borrow or kidnap whenever I have the chance."

"Come from a big family?"

"If I told you how big, you probably wouldn't believe it. My mother's been divorced four times—at last count—and my dad's on his third wife. My background hasn't given me much faith in the institution of marriage, but I've collected whole clans of relatives along the way. In fact, I developed this theory, growing up."

"Yeah?" He hadn't a clue where she was leading, but if it was going to make her eyes sparkle and dance like that, he was willing to hear anything.

"Yeah. As a kid, I couldn't see a reason on earth why I had to lose all my relatives because of divorce. I mean *they* were getting divorces. I wasn't. So I decided to keep the relatives I was fond of. My aunt Betty, for instance, was a blood relative, but she was always a pistol. When she divorced my uncle Henry, I kept him. And my mom's second husband's parents—I've kept them as honorary grandparents. And then there are people like Jeanne—she's a writer—she was my dad's first wife's niece... your eyes are crossing, Josh, are you getting a little confused?"

Damned if she wasn't teasing him. "I'm just trying to picture who you have over for dinner on the holidays," he said dryly. "The idea that you can keep or throw out the relatives you want is a little...unusual."

"Families don't seem to exist like they used to. If that's the way it's going to be, I figure we'll have to create our nuclear-age families out of a new mold. And you're divorced, so you already know how complicated it can get for the kids around birthdays and holidays—which ex-aunts and uncles get invited for which occasions—"

"Yeah, it gets complicated." But his mind, for the first time in a millennium, wasn't on his children. It was on her.

Vaguely he recalled that his sole reason for coming here had been to talk about Killer. Vaguely he recalled the madhouse of chores and noise and kids that he needed to go home to—soon. Yet he'd stretched out his legs. He couldn't remember when. Her place, the warmth of lamplight and quiet and soft blues, gave him the strange feeling of being in a spellbound cocoon. When was the last time he'd shared a basic conversation with a woman? When was the last time a woman had curled up across from him, and focused her attention on his face as if nothing else mattered in the world except the conversation between the two of them?

"It's hard to believe you mean that—about being antimarriage. Maybe the odds of a couple staying together aren't too hot today. And just having been through a divorce, I get a case of hives even thinking about wedding rings again. But you must have been tempted to get married sometime. And if you want kids..."

"I want kids. But I'd never get married just for that reason. There's no stigma against being a single mom these days. Obviously the situation is better for a child with both a mom and dad, but a ring doesn't guarantee that."

He argued with her. A damn silly argument, considering that nobody knew better than him how little a ring guaranteed. But it was fun, bickering the pros and cons of marriage back and forth with her. Eventually they moved off marriage and tried out an argument about politics—no way they could agree on anything there; she was a flaming do-gooder liberal, which he could have guessed. But they weren't really fighting. She kept laughing, and making him laugh. She had a hatful of free-spirited wild ideas about life and love and everything else. Josh couldn't begin to guess if she was serious, nor did it matter. For the first time in forever, he wasn't thinking about work or bills or kids or when he was going to find time to change the oil on his Bronco.

But damn. When his gaze accidentally flickered to the dials on his watch, he almost had a stroke. How could he possibly have been there two hours?

He lurched to his feet faster than a bee-stung bear. "Damn. I didn't realize how late it was. And I never meant to take up your whole evening."

"I didn't mind. I enjoyed talking with you."

"Yeah...I enjoyed it, too." Belatedly he realized how true that was, how much fun he'd had over the past two hours...and it worried him.

Ariel trailed him into the blue-and-white kitchen. "I'll get your jacket. Hopefully it'll be dry by now."

She glanced out the black windows. "It's still drizzling, but I haven't heard a boomer in a while. Looks like the worst of the storm finally passed."

She fetched his denim jacket from the minuscule entryway and held it up with a smile.

"Thanks," he said. It only took a second to put on his boots and yank on the jacket. Then he meant to reach for the doorknob and go. There was no reason his leaving her had to be complicated.

But somehow he found himself still standing there. Close to her. Awkwardly close. In her bare feet, she reached his nose in height. With the sink light behind her, her delicate features were less shadowed than simply softened, blurred. Feminine scents seemed to surround her. Not one, but a blend—mango from her shampoo, and peach from the hand cream he'd seen her reach for, and yeah, he could catch an exotic spice from the perfume where her skin was warm. Her skin looked real, real warm.

When he'd first walked in, his tongue had been tangled somewhere near the roof of his mouth. Studying her over the evening, he'd seen she was pale. Too pale. And she had a plain old ordinary chin. Discovering those imperfections had been a relief. No way a guy could have a normal conversation with his personal Christie Brinkley fantasy. But she wasn't that now. The legs, the body, the sultry green eyes—it was all still there, all just as distracting. But somehow over the evening she'd become... real.

And she looked at him, impossibly, as if she found him real, too. "You're not really going to ground Killer for the rest of her life, are you?" she queried.

"I haven't a clue what I'm gonna do with her," he admitted dryly. "But thanks... for not being mad about her taking those things. And just . . . for listening.''

"No problem," she said lightly.

"Well . . . good night."

"Good night," she returned.

He reached for the door. So did she. Their hands brushed, making them both chuckle.

They both jumped back to give the other room, making them both chuckle again.

And then their eyes met. And the most confounding thing happened.

Three

———

All evening, Josh had the weird sensation that it was wicked and wrong to be alone with her. His six-year-old was having trouble handling the temptation of Ariel's magic. He wasn't afraid of crystal balls or card tricks, but yeah, he was uncomfortably aware that the lady had some kind of magic. Dangerous magic, because she sure as hell seemed to have cast some kind of spell on him.

For that reason alone, he never meant to kiss her. He'd have sworn in court that neither the thought nor intent was remotely on his mind. And a guy was supposed to be able to count on those handy physics laws of the universe—like the relationship between fire and fuel. If nobody lit a match, nobody had to worry about the repercussions of starting a blaze.

There were no matches in sight. There was just an instant—an innocent instant—when they were standing together in her shadowed doorway. Her face was tilted up to his. He was wearing his denim jacket, ready to leave, his hand even on the doorknob. Their eyes met. It couldn't have been for more than a millisecond. Nobody made a soul connection in a millisecond. For cripes' sake, Josh didn't even believe in hoaxy ethereal stuff like "soul connections."

But *something* happened. Something insane. Something that made it feel perfectly natural to lift his hand to gently touch her cheek. When she turned her head, he bent down, as if they already naturally knew the steps to this dance. When their lips met, though, there was nothing natural about the kiss.

Her lips were softer than butter. Softer than spring. Her eyes turned this smoky misty green, and then they closed, as if inhaling the texture of this sensation was all she could concentrate on. She tasted sweet, and to kiss her small mouth, her lips, was like sliding on silk.

Hormones. His mind lanced on the word, seeking excuses and explanations for an explosion of emotion that had no such simple reason. Yeah, his whole body tightened from the chemical connection. And below his belt, he knew exactly what she was doing to him.

But that crazy, wild kiss had nothing of lust in it. It was a lost kiss. A testing, tentative, beguiling acknowledgment of longing and loneliness.

He'd never denied being lonely; it was just supposed to be a back-burner item, a problem he'd take out and deal with after the kids were grown and he had time for it. Only, she put it on his table right now. How many nights he'd been alone. How fiercely he missed believing there would ever be someone to talk to, be with. How rich, how heady, how mountain-tall a man could feel with a woman who cared about him.

He wasn't used to riches—not extravagant, expensive, luxurious riches like her. Her silk rustled alluringly against his denim. His callused hands seemed an impossible contrast against her pearl skin. The pulse was beating hard in her throat. Hard, but not fast. The whole world had tuned down to slow motion, as if life had been kind enough to give them both a time-out, and nothing existed, not at this moment, but the two of them and a kiss that neither of them could seem to let go of.

He'd wondered how that long hair would feel sifting through his hands. Now he knew. Dangerous. A man's fingers could get lost in those long, shivery strands and never come out. Her hands clutched his jacket and then slid, softly and slowly, around his neck.

Somewhere, he could smell blueberry muffins. Somewhere, he could hear a clock ticking. Somewhere, a coat hook was stabbing him directly between the shoulder blades, and it was extremely odd, but he didn't give a damn. She was kissing him back as though she hadn't met a man who mattered to her in the past four, five thousand years. His instincts pitched back to the caveman era, but even accounting for those primitive, prehistoric male emotions, he knew damn well he'd never kissed anyone like her. The crush of her plump breasts made him feel hot and violently protective at the same time. Her skin warmed under his touch—warmed and flushed. Her scent, her texture and touch, hit him like a seductive, erotic overload.

He tried to gulp in oxygen.

There wasn't a lick of air in the whole room.

She tried to gulp in air, too, then raised her eyes and smiled at him as if she were waking from some dream. "Josh?"

He wasn't sure what she was asking. Her voice was husky, low, shy. Hurtable, he recognized. Never mind her sensual feminine lair and her antimarriage rhetoric and the free spirit implied by her walking around in pajamas. She didn't do this every day.

Hell, neither did he.

It took a second to untangle his hands from her hair, to smooth a strand away from her face, to brush his lips against her brow. The kiss was a gesture of comfort, not apology. He couldn't apologize for something he wasn't sorry for. But he also couldn't talk about something he couldn't explain.

She seemed to understand, seemed in no mood for conversation, either, because she smiled at him just before he turned around and pulled open the door.

Outside, a cool drizzling rain was still falling. He yanked up his collar and headed down the slick, wet metal steps. Smells drifted off the Connecticut River; a passing car swished water from a puddle, but that was the only sound. The whole town was dark and quiet. The white steeple of the Congregational Church and pointed rooftops were familiar landmarks, everything washed and clean this night. Rainbows haloed under the street lamps as he climbed into the cool, damp seat of the Bronco. He lifted up to filch the key from his jeans pocket and started the engine.

And then he took a breath. It seemed the first lungful of real oxygen he'd had since being with her.

For some crazy reason, that spellbound feeling didn't want to go away. Josh had no patience or belief in fairy dust. He didn't exactly *mind* a singular, temporary, short, one-shot excursion into insanity...surely any guy was entitled? Every male human being had fantasies from the day he reached puberty, but he never expected to actually experience one. Ariel. Hell. If all those looks and sensuality and sex appeal weren't enough to knock a guy to his knees, her openness and giving nature, the way she listened as if he were the only man in the universe—and yeah, the way she kissed—were enough to rattle any man.

Of *course* he was shook up.

It was okay that he was shook up. No reason to panic. It was probably underlined and italicized in the guys' rule book somewhere—any male exposed to Ariel Lindstrom who was not shook up should probably run, not walk, to a doctor for an immediate physical.

It was just that nothing like that had ever happened to him before.

He turned at the light, cruised Maple for a block, then traveled up the hill into his little burb. If it hadn't been storming earlier, he'd have walked to her shop. The drive didn't take five minutes.

The kids had left the lights on. In fact—no surprise, with him gone—every window in the house was ablaze with lights. The month's electric bill was gonna be a monster. He swiped a hand over his face as he locked the Bronco and loped to the back door. It was coming back. Sanity. Slowly, too slowly, but logic and common sense had never deserted Josh for long.

A moment's craziness was understandable, even acceptable. As long as a guy didn't mistake it for reality.

The reality was that he had three troubled kids, a work and life schedule that blitzed any free time, and a mess of a divorce behind him. What would she want with a ready-made household of trouble, dirty towels, dishes and a kleptomaniac squirt? No way, nohow, could he picture Ariel fitting in. No way could he picture any sane woman wanting to.

He was in no position to ask any woman in his life. And that was that.

He'd call. Ariel was sure he'd call. The secret, heady, champagne-high feeling of anticipation lasted for three days.

She never expected anything monumental. She never had—not from men or relationships. All her life she'd been an enthusiastic defender of magic, but that was never because she couldn't tell the difference between fantasy and reality. She had no faith in forevers, but a body could still seek—and reach for—those rare and real magical moments in life.

The evening with Josh had been magical. Special. There was no doubt in her mind that he felt the same way. They'd talked as easily and naturally as kindred spirits. He'd looked so stiff and tired when he first walked in, but she'd slowly watched him unbend, unfold, relax. Other men had looked at her with desire, but she'd never sensed a predator-and-prey feeling with Josh. The excitement he'd inspired had been wicked and nerve tingling, but not really threatening. She'd never have gone in his arms if she were afraid of him. She never remembered experiencing a kiss quite like that. It was like skydiving off a star, free-falling in the darkness to a place where she felt dizzyingly protected and desired and cherished all at once.

She'd kissed her share of men in the past decade. Never had a kiss or a man felt so right. And she wasn't presuming to know Josh's feelings, but positively he couldn't have power-packed that kind of tenderness and raw emotion in an embrace if he hadn't shared some of those feelings.

Only he hadn't called the next day.

Or the next night.

Or the next day.

Three days had passed now, though, and that heady feeling of anticipation had fizzled out like too-long-uncorked champagne. Apparently she'd been wrong. Embarrassingly wrong. The only one doing any emotional skydiving must have been her, because it was hurtfully obvious that he wasn't interested.

The telephone rang, but she ignored it. New stock had just arrived; she was buried neck-deep in boxes, and Dot was out front and would surely catch the call. Seconds later, though, her partner's head poked around the doorway. "It's for you. Mason."

Grateful for the distraction, she wiped her dusty hands on a rag and hustled for the phone. Mason, an English professor in Boston, had been her one foray into trying out a forever. They'd lived together for three years. No different than any other relationship, that delightful spin of first love hadn't lasted, but they'd managed to call it quits and still stay friends. Good friends.

"I haven't heard from you in two weeks, you piker. Whatcha been up to?"

Mason was "up to" a deliriously happy love affair with a woman named Suzanna. He wasn't getting any work done. He was losing weight, couldn't eat, had given up sleep, was having trouble remembering his own name.

"This sounds *wonderful*. She's really something, huh?" Dragging the phone cord, Ariel reached in the back room minirefrigerator and snatched a soda. No way to open it single-handed. She trapped the receiver between her ear and shoulder, so she had both hands to flip open the lid. "I don't want to hear how gorgeous she is, you doofus. Who cares. Is she *nice?* What does she do, how'd you meet her, what kinds of things have you two been doing together . . . ?"

Ariel had never quite figured out why the lovelorn sought her advice, since she never made a secret of her chosen single life-style. She'd been an advice-giver for so long that she rarely thought about it. But Mason was winding up to a long dissertation—and she'd guzzled half her ginger ale—when she abruptly realized that she wasn't alone.

Josh may have dismissed her from his personal map, but apparently his offspring hadn't.

Killer was standing on one foot, a balancing act apparently designed to give her something to do when she was stuck being patient. Her tennies were powder pink today. One of her lopsided pigtails sported a green polka dot bow, and her fingernails were painted a startling hellion-red shade, most of which was bitten off. Hopeful chocolate eyes were peeled on Ariel.

Behind her were two boys, standing still as statues. In no sense were they a physically matched set, but they definitely had a few things in common—slicked back hair, cowlicks, gawky arms and legs, and a terrified look of adolescent self-consciousness. One glance at their eyes, and Ariel would have bet the bank who their daddy was.

"Mason, catch you later, okay? Something's come up. I'll call you back." She hung up the receiver and turned around. "Hi, sweetie."

"Hi, Ariel. Did you see how quiet I was while you were on the phone? Are you still busy?"

"Yes, I saw how quiet you were—and nope, I'm not busy at all."

"Good, 'cause my brothers didn't believe me about you. And Dad said I couldn't come here any more unless I was...supravised. So I brought everybody to meet you. This is Calvin and this is Bruiser and this is Boober."

Ariel extended her palm to Calvin, who flushed beet red for the handshake. He was going to be eight feet tall if he ever finished growing, she guessed, but temporarily he was stuck with big feet and a cracking voice and arms that were just too long to know what to do with themselves. "She's not supposed to bother you," he said, with a shoulder hunch in the direction of Killer.

"There's no bothering involved. Patrice and I are old pals," Ariel assured him, and then extended a hand to Bruiser. "That's not your real name, is it?"

"Nah. My real name's Daniel, but I take wrestling, you know? So everybody calls me Bruiser."

"I can see why," she said gravely. Although the muscles weren't that developed yet, the attitude was all there, from the swaggering posture to the fingers dug into his jeans pockets. He was maybe thirteen? And he'd had peanut butter for lunch, judging from the teensy bit stuck on his chin. She wasn't about to tell him what that peanut butter did to his tough-guy persona. "Nice to meet you, Bruiser, and this is Boober, huh?"

Remembering that Killer's imaginary friend was of legendary height, Ariel looked way up as she extended her hand into thin air. "Nice to meet you, too, Boober." She duly pumped the air as if there were actually a handshake involved. Both boys rolled their eyes at her foolishness, but they didn't seem to mind her catering to their sister. She could see a little of those terrible self-aware nerves fading.

"Killer said you knew magic tricks and stuff." Calvin, cracked voice and all, had apparently been voted spokesman. "Not that we're interested. We're too old for stuff like that. But she was driving us crazy, and I don't have to deliver papers for a coupla hours, so we just kind of thought we'd take a walk. And we accidentally ended up here. But if we're in your way or anything..."

"You're not in my way," Ariel immediately denied. The day she was too busy for kids would never happen. Too many adults had made her feel "in the way" when she was growing up.

Still, what to do with the Penoyer clan was trickier than a land mine. Josh's silence had clearly spelled out his lack of interest in any personal connection with her. Maybe he didn't want his kids involved with her, either?

Killer elbowed her brother. "I told you she was cool, didn't I?"

Cool. Ariel's heart sank. How the Sam Hill could she live up to an impossible kid epithet like *cool?* And there was no way she bought Calvin's story about "accidentally" stopping by. Positively she was being checked out with more studying interest than a crammer in exam week. Bruiser, the poor kid, couldn't keep his eyes off her breasts. Calvin hovered more at a distance, his eyes examining her face, her hair and how she behaved, as if prepared to abscond with his brother and sister any second if she did anything suspicious.

She handed out cans of soda. That broke some ice. Bruiser caught a look at her jewelry tools on the counter. That started him talking. And then Calvin, who denied his interest in magic loudly several times, was eventually coaxed into trying out some sleight-of-hand coin tricks.

The clan leveled her dried-out potato chips and pop supply in less than an hour. Customers started flowing in the store then. Dot was out front, and Dot could probably handle a football stadium crowd single-handedly, but Calvin picked up that Ariel was distracted. "Okay, that's enough. We gotta go. I got papers to deliver and Bruiser's still gotta mow the lawn before Dad gets home. I may buy that nesting shells trick, not for me, you know, but I have a friend who's real interested in stuff like that . . . if it's okay?"

"It's okay," Ariel told him. She rang up the sale with all three crowding closer than shadows, examining everything from the antique cash register to all the supplies behind the counter.

"You got a safe," Bruiser said.

"Of course she's got a safe, you nitwit. This is a store. Come on, we gotta go."

"I don't *want* to go, Calvin. I want to stay here."

"Yeah, well, your vote doesn't count for nothing because you're just a little squirt." The words were big-brother mean, but he swung his sister on his shoulders, just like Josh carried her. Even so, Killer's lower lip started to tremble. "I got a sucker in my pocket. You cry, you get nothing," Calvin warned her.

"I won't cry."

"So how come you're already starting to pucker, crybaby?"

"I'm not. I'm not. I'm not crying at all and I *hate* you for saying I'm a crybaby...." Patrice hesitated. "What color sucker?"

Ariel watched the trio leave, talking six for the dozen as they passed by the storefront window. Dot, arms folded over her ample chest, glanced at the kids and then took a long look at her partner. "Didn't take long for you to lose your heart."

"They're special kids," Ariel said defensively.

Dot blew her nose with a noisy honk. "There isn't a child born that you don't think is special. You've been picking up strays for as long as I've known you, but I'm not sure who was adopting who there, kiddo. Those three were really looking you over. Offhand, I'd guess they were window-shopping for a new mom."

"Come on. You know how often kids come in here. They all love the magic tricks. It has nothing to do with me personally."

"You think not?" Dot shook her head. "I'd bet those three aren't talking about buying any magic tricks—they're talking about putting you on layaway."

Customers were waiting; they both surged forward to take care of them, but the conversation lingered in Ariel's mind. She hoped Dot was wrong. Her store was in the neighborhood; she couldn't, wouldn't, discourage any of the local kids from stopping in. She'd meant to be both friendly and kind to Josh's brood...but not if they realized how uniquely her heart felt drawn to them.

Ariel remembered, too well, being little and lonely and confused after every one of her parents' divorces. She would never willingly be part of building a child's unreasonable expectations about anything. She wasn't stepmom material.

Which their father had apparently already figured out real well.

"So...whatcha want for dinner?" Josh asked his youngest.

"Macaroni-and-cheese."

"Now, there's a shock to my heart." He opened up the cupboard, where twenty boxes of macaroni-and-cheese were neatly stacked within easy reach. Who ever said a dad couldn't anticipate the six-year-old female mind? He filled a pan with water, then dumped in the macaroni. The directions claimed you were supposed to wait until the water boiled, but what the hey. Eventually it all got cooked. "The next question is what you want to go with it."

"Peanut-butter-and-marshmallow sandwiches," Patrice said promptly.

"Now, Killer, you know I love you. But once a week is all I can take of that. How about a nice juicy steak grilled outside on the barbecue?"

"Yuck."

"How about some disgusting, terrible-for-you chicken?" Josh regarded his youngest hopefully. Sometimes that lying thing worked. By trying to convince the kids that chicken and fish were bad for them, he could occasionally build up interest and desire. Not this time.

"Boober and I want peanut-butter-and-marsh-mallow sandwiches or *nothing,* Daddy."

"Yeah? Well, I've about had it with our pretending this Boober is real, squirt, when you know darn well he isn't.... Bruiser! Your turn to set the table. Calvin!" He lifted Killer to the counter by the sink. Her official dinner chore was salad making, because she liked to shred the lettuce and pour on the croutons.

"Can we watch *Aladdin* together tonight?"

Josh considered whether he would survive the five hundredth replay of *Aladdin.* The answer was no. He wouldn't. He really wouldn't. He'd always been prepared for the tough parenting jobs, illness, value teaching, that sort of thing. But nobody ever told him that moms put up with six-year-old nonstop talking. Or how much patience it took to braid silky-fine hair. Or how a sane human being was supposed to endure five million hours of nonstop Disney. "Sure," he said.

Calvin showed up in the doorway. "Did you get the wash out of the dryer?" Josh asked.

"I was going to do it after dinner."

And cows flew. "The way I remember it, you wanted out tonight to play pinball with your pals. Chores first, or nobody's going anywhere."

"Dad, doing wash is a *girl's* job. I took out the trash."

"We all gave up trying to iron, didn't we? I don't care if we're wrinkled, but no way we're going around in dirty clothes. And that means everybody has to pitch in. I can't put in ten-hour workdays and get everything else in the house done."

Josh could see Calvin was debating giving him lip. Ever since he'd turned fourteen, challenging parental authority had become a full-time sport. Josh could remember testing his own dad the same way, but that didn't make coping with the problem any easier. The dinner hour was predictably as peaceful as a holiday in the Middle East.

Two glasses of milk spilled. That was par. Silverware dropped and clattered. Killer got her sandwich; the steaks were overburned but edible. The fight over whose turn it was to do the dishes began early and threatened to turn into a shouting match. Then the boys started shooting peas with their spoons...sheesh, he had to quit serving peas. It wasn't like anybody ate vegetables anyway.

He could handle a construction crew, face whole days where nothing at work went right and still come through loving the challenge. But nothing exhausted him faster than the short hour at dinner.

"We're the only people who do this, you know," Bruiser complained.

"Do what?"

"Eat together. Billy's mom gives him money to go get McDonald's. Steve gets to order pizza whenever he wants, because none of his family's ever home. *Nobody* actually sits around and eats together anymore, Dad."

Somewhere in that disgusted complaint, Josh thought, there was almost a compliment. "Well, we're not other people. And we're going to keep eating together like a family. Even if it kills us.... What'd you three do today? Anything special?"

Sudden silence. All eyes focused on plates. Josh felt his stomach clench in immediate paternal panic.

"Well, I washed the car. And played a little one-on-one in Harry's backyard," Bruiser finally volunteered.

"Yeah? And?"

"And we took Killer on a little walk. She was bored, you know, with the baby-sitter not here today and all. We wandered down to that store that sells magic tricks. You don't have to worry. We watched the squirt real close." Calvin cleared his throat. "She's a helluva looker, Dad."

"Don't say hell in front of your sister."

"*You* do," Calvin pointed out.

"Well, I'm trying not to. We all need to work at cleaning up our language—"

Bruiser interrupted. "She really is something."

"Who?" Why he asked the question was beyond Josh. The answer was no surprise.

"Ms. Lindstrom. Ariel. I mean, the other day, we all couldn't help but notice that you spent half the night at her place...."

"I spent a couple of hours there. Part of an evening. For a very good reason—"

Calvin intervened before his brother could say anything else. "Sure. We know. Everything's copacetic, Dad, not to get your liver in an uproar. We just wanted a look at her, you know? And she's cool. That's all we're saying. We liked her okay."

Josh opened his mouth...and closed it. The nerve of his three monsters boggled his mind. He knew they missed their mother and the subject of his dating had come up before. All three considered themselves qualified to offer him advice. Even the pipsqueak. As if dad's love life—or lack of it—was a public subject requiring audience participation.

He was raising them wrong, he thought glumly. His parents had set up a nice, repressive household where nobody dared express temper or opinions. Repression—discipline—kept everybody in line, so how come he couldn't master it as a parent himself? He mentally pictured his two oldest devils walking into Ariel's place, checking her out, what she must have thought, what she must have felt. And considered taking cyanide.

Chairs scraped back. Dishes were carted to the counter. Josh obliterated Ariel from his mind, the same way he'd chased her out of his thoughts all week now. He likened her to the flu. Once a man caught the symptoms, denial was a waste of breath, but eventually the problem went away. A grown man just had to tough it out.

He "toughed out" sitting through *Aladdin* with Killer, fixed the leaky faucet in the upstairs bathroom and spent a confounded hour with the dryer—which he was convinced ate socks. By eleven the house was quiet. Bruiser had sacked out early. Calvin, his night owl, was still up but entranced in front of a computer screen with some sci-fi game. Killer had developed an appalling new habit of waking up with nightmares and stealing into his bed in the middle of the night, but temporarily she was sleeping like an angel.

Josh locked up and started turning off lights, automatically picking up stuff on his route upstairs. Calvin's jacket that had fallen on the floor. Bruiser's exercise equipment that had been left in the middle of the living room. And Killer's shoes—Killer had a collection of tennis shoes that kept reproducing by osmosis, as far as Josh could tell. When he lifted the pair of pale pink tennies to carry them upstairs, though, something jingled.

He peered into the toe, frowned, then dug his hand in. A pair of earrings dropped into his palm. Long things, dangly, sterling with a bunch of itty-bitty glittery stones. Expensive. The earrings had those hook things for pierced ears.

His six-year-old didn't have pierced ears.

His six-year-old also didn't own a pair of earrings.

Four

———

Ariel was just climbing out of the tub when the telephone rang. She snatched a towel and flew. Although she'd lost track of time in the bathtub, it had to be past eleven. Awfully late for a chitchat call, but heaven knew, her life was full of honorary relatives who could develop a problem at any hour.

Breathless—and still dripping wet—she grabbed the receiver in the bedroom by the fourth ring. "Hello?"

"Ariel? It's Josh." The masculine tenor abruptly tacked on "Penoyer" as if he thought she might need the last name to distinguish him from the other Joshes in her life.

There were no other Joshes in her life. Nor did she need any last-name tag to recognize the roll and pitch of that uniquely masculine voice. "Hi."

She dropped the towel, picked it up again, then forgot all about drying herself and sank on the edge of the bed. She glanced at the clock, but the time didn't register. She stared at the emerald-green sheets and down comforter, but nothing seemed familiar in the room in that instant, either. Her mind tumbled around a dozen chaotic thoughts, but only one connected— oh, God, she should have expected this call. "You're angry with me, right? About your kids coming to see me?"

"Angry? No, that's not why—"

"Honestly, Josh, I didn't know they were coming. And I kept thinking how awkward you'd feel if you'd realized they planned that visit. It was sweet, really, the way the boys were checking me out. I mean, it showed how much they loved you, how protective they felt about their dad. So that visit was really a compliment to what great kids you're raising. There's no reason to feel awkward—"

"Ariel . . . um . . . that's not exactly why I was calling—"

She could hear him clearing his throat. He was so obviously one of those men who got real nervous trying to talk about feelings. "Look. I know we don't know each other well enough for you to trust me, but I promise there was no problem. When you didn't call the other night . . . well, I got the message. We had a good time talking the other night, but it was nothing you wanted to pursue. No sweat. I understand. But even if I hadn't gotten the message that you weren't interested, I would never—*never*—have given your kids the idea that the two of us were . . . well . . ."

"Ariel, is there even a slim, remote possibility that maybe you'd let me get a word in here?"

"Of course," she said gently. "I just wanted you to know that I wouldn't have encouraged your kids to believe we were a couple. Or that I had any involvement in their lives. It happened to me too often growing up, Josh. Potential stepdads and stepmoms using me as a go-between. I feel really violently about it—"

"She took your earrings."

"—I would never say anything to a child that would build up unrealistic expectations. I'd shoot myself first. I'm always really careful with kids, not to..." Her voice trailed off. She suddenly flopped flat on the comforter with a hand over her eyes. "She took *what* earrings?"

"You didn't know you were missing some earrings? Sterling silver, long jangly things, little red stones that I hope to God aren't rubies."

"Killer? Took those earrings? *That's* what you're calling for?"

"Afraid so."

"Well geezle beezle. Did I just embarrass myself to death telling you all that other stuff?"

"No." Josh cleared his throat. Again. "I'd been thinking about all that, too. It was kind of a relief when you put it all on the table." She heard the sound of a door closing. "I was considering strangling my sons. Boiling them in oil. Hanging them out in the rain by their toenails. They've both got more nerves than brains. I was having a fit that they'd embarrassed you."

"Actually, I loved them," she said frankly.

"Well, actually, I love them, too. Even when I'm mad enough to strangle them. But it's my third offspring who seems to be giving me the most fits. It seems I need to be returning this pair of earrings. I have to work late tomorrow—"

"You want to bring them by my apartment after that?"

"No." He rejected that idea faster than a scissor snap. "That is, if you don't mind going somewhere else. I was wondering if you'd let me buy you a drink. The Brown Jug—you know the place? Like around seven. Tomorrow night."

"A drink?"

"A drink." He defined the word as if he were afraid it was unfamiliar. "Like a beer. Or a glass of wine."

She knew what a drink was. She'd just never expected the offer to come from Josh. "Well...sure. That's okay with me."

"Maybe it's a bad idea. If you mind going to a bar—"

"No problem," she said.

Seconds later, they both cut off the conversation. Eventually, she got around to hanging up the towel, pulling on a nightgown and turning off her apartment lights. Even after snuggling between the emerald-green sheets, though, she still felt bewildered by the whole conversation.

If any other single man had asked her for a drink, she'd have made certain assumptions. Not with him. Josh had been stiff and nervous through the whole phone call. Hell's bells, there'd been a thread of panic in his voice when she'd suggested meeting at her place.

The outrageous thought drifted through her mind that he was afraid of her.

The idea barely surfaced before she chuckled in the darkness. Punching the pillow, she tugged the comforter close around her neck and closed her eyes. Josh had the physical muscular look of a man who could take out a street mugger in three seconds flat. There was no conceivable way he could see her as any kind of emotional or physical threat to him. She was beat. So tired-whipped-beat that her brain was functioning on silly power.

He just wanted to return the earrings and had picked a place to do it. Fear had nothing to do with it. The idea was so beyond silly that she chuckled again just before falling asleep.

Talk about terror. As Josh leapt down from the Bronco, his palms were sweating and his throat was drier than a desert cave. As a kid, he'd been scared of snakes. As a teenager, he remembered being cornered by three bullies in the school gym locker room. As a man, he remembered stripping down in front of his first lover.

So it wasn't as though he'd never experienced terror before.

He just remembered it as being a lot easier to handle than this.

He tucked in his shirt and straightened his collar. Then just stood there. He checked his watch. The dial had only moved a snail-slow thirty seconds since the last time he'd looked. It wasn't seven yet. He'd deliberately arrived early, expecting to wait—no way a lady should have to walk in a bar alone.

The door to the Brown Jug opened, revealing a comforting array of sights and sounds. Three guys spilled out, dressed in jeans and construction boots, just like him. The inside was already filled with smoke and rowdy laughter and the snapping sound of billiard balls connecting.

There was nothing rough or dangerous about the bar. It was a place for blue-collar workers to hang out after a long day. Josh wasn't much for hanging out in bars, but he knew the place, knew most of the faces.

Ariel, he figured, was going to fit in like a butterfly in a barn. He'd never chosen the place to make Ariel feel uncomfortable. He just wanted a meeting on his turf.

He was not only positive, but determined that she'd look different to him in familiar surroundings. There was no chance a man's hormones could get ahead of him in a public place like this. There was no way a man could get confused by soft lights and quiet and the feminine sensual promise he saw—or thought he saw—in a dangerous pair of winsome green eyes.

He straightened his collar. Again. He'd be safe here. She'd be safe here. Everybody would be safe here; he'd be able to return those damn earrings in five minutes flat; they'd share a fast drink and he would be home no later than eight.

Nothing to be scared of.

A snazzy little red MG rode into the lot and braked to a jolting stop in a far parking space. Adrenaline pumped through his veins faster than an alcoholic guzzling whiskey.

She climbed out of the expensive little Midget with her bare legs swinging. Obviously she'd spotted him waiting, because she headed straight for him. "Hi, Josh! I'm not late, am I? I had a little trouble finding the place, but I hope I didn't keep you waiting long."

"No problem, I just got here myself." His pulse rate was bouncing like a teeter-totter. He'd been right about the butterfly in the barn thing—she didn't have a prayer of fitting in with his construction crowd—but he'd counted on her allure for him disappearing in comfortingly familiar surroundings.

No cigar. Technically she was dressed casually, as far as the jeans skirt and sandals, but she was just one of those women who was doomed to look exotic and elegant. The silky scarf at her neck, the cloisonné bangle on her wrist, the unignorably lush sweep of silvery blond hair held back by a matching cloisonné comb... hell, her smile alone had a life-threatening effect on his blood pressure. "This place isn't real fancy," he warned her.

"Well, that's good, because I hate real fancy." Her eyes danced humorously. "I'm about to die of thirst, though. We're not going to have a problem finding something cool and wet, are we?"

Her mouth looked cool and wet. Enough to give a man a killing thirst—if a man weren't dead determined to be a total gentleman. "Let's get you inside. Shouldn't take long to get a drink ordered."

He steered her through the crowd with a protective hand at the small of her back, dead-eyed every masculine gaze that shot in her direction and led her to a quiet booth. Several guys yelled out a "Hey, Josh!" or a "Long time no see" or a "How come you been such a stranger!"

The bartender, Harry Lamoza, slapped a bowl of pretzels and peanuts on the table, took his order for the house tap and winked at Josh when Ariel thoughtfully ordered a peach daiquiri. The bar never lacked for women customers, but it had probably been a blue moon since anyone ordered a truly sissy "girl drink."

"Everyone seems to know you," Ariel commented.

"I don't come in here much any more. Too many reasons to get home quick after work. Like my kids.

But a lot of people here are from the old neighborhood where I grew up, and I run across quite a few of them on different jobs.''

"They look like a nice bunch of guys.''

"They are.'' Somehow he hadn't expected her to see it. At first glance, the range of ethnic accents and rough-and-tumble faces would hardly make a woman think of "class.'' Some of the old clan had cut him when he'd climbed the ranks to boss—not a popular status with this union crew—but most of them were the salt of the earth. They'd come around when Nancy left him, just like he'd stood by them through some rough waters. "Somehow I wouldn't think you'd have much reason to be around many construction guys.''

"Nope. Grew up in a really academic atmosphere. Old Philadelphia. Pendleton and pearls.'' She scooped up a handful of peanuts. "Still, I never find that people are really different anywhere. Different trappings, maybe. But everyone seems to go through the same life trials, same problems. And there's about the same proportion of turkeys and good hearts anywhere you live—''

Harry interrupted when he delivered the drinks. It had to be a stomach-challenging blend—peach daiquiri and peanuts. But she kept scooping up those peanuts and sipping. Josh could see right off that she was a real drinker. At the rate she was sipping, she just might finish that drink four months from Thursday.

He could have hustled her along. He meant to. The whole setup should have been perfect. A peach daiquiri drinker from a Pendleton-and-pearls background—sheesh, this should have been easy; the two of them had as much in common as a Rottweiler and a French poodle. One short miserably awkward conversation and they could both escape each other's company zippedy quick.

All too soon he realized—dismally—that wasn't going to happen. He returned her earrings right away, of course. And he apologized sincerely, because he unquestionably owed her a sincere apology. But that was supposed to be it.

Just like that strange night at her place, though, Ariel sabotaged him. The damn woman was mortifyingly easy to talk to. And she listened. And as if there weren't thirty other guys in the room, she focused on him as if he were the only man in the universe. Josh never aired his private linen. He sure as hell never burdened a stranger with his problems. It *had* to be her fault that he couldn't quit talking.

"You're the only one she's stealing from. Killer's never done anything like this before. I don't get it— why she's doing this, why she's picked on you or what the hell I'm supposed to do about it as her dad."

"You think this could have something to do with her mother leaving?" Ariel asked quietly.

"Hell, I know it does. Ever since Nancy split, there's been one thing after another. Her latest thing is nightmares, waking up scared, climbing into bed with me in the middle of the night." Josh rubbed the back of his neck. "A few months ago, I tried taking her to a counselor."

"That didn't help?"

"Killer accused the woman of having a pea brain and stinking of rat perfume."

"Oh, Lord, I can picture Killer saying that." Ariel chuckled, but her eyes softened with warmth and concern. "I take it the two of them didn't get along."

"About as well as a snake and mongoose. Maybe I should have looked for somebody else, but damn, I never needed any highfalutin' psychologist to tell me that my daughter's feeling angry and rejected because her mother split. Killer won't even talk to Nancy. She doesn't want a mother who doesn't want her. In time, I think she'll come around. The boys have. We're still a family, even if Nancy isn't there, which the boys seem to understand. It's just Patrice.... At the rate she's going, she's gonna have a police record before her seventh birthday."

"Now, come on. I hardly think this brief foray into shoplifting means she's going to end up in reform school, Josh."

"No? I've tried grounding her for life and forbidding her near your shop. And both the baby-sitter and the boys are supposed to watch out for her. So far, nothing's working. But I was thinking—"

"What?"

Josh gulped a sip of beer, and abruptly wondered where his head was. Poughkeepsie? Kansas? Somehow he'd gotten lost between the empathy in the soft green eyes and the dangerous, distracting allure of all those warm smiles. It wasn't like him to take a wrong turn. He'd been spilling out all this stuff as if he knew her. "Look...I didn't mean to run on. None of this is your problem."

"Maybe not, in the sense that I have any right to interfere. But somehow I've become part of the problem, wouldn't you say? If Patrice is acting a certain way because of me? At least tell me what you were going to say," she prodded him.

"Well...that's what I saw, too. That she's developed this fascination with you, quoting you night and day, how you know magic, how you dress, what you say. I'm not saying you're at fault for anything—you're not. But the squirt seems determined to catch your attention, and I'm getting nowhere trying to keep her out of your hair. Hell, I don't want to put you on the spot. Believe me, I'd understand if you said no...."

When his voice trailed off, Ariel leaned forward and folded her arms on the table. "Josh?"

"What?"

"I haven't a clue what you're trying to ask me, but if you don't just get it out and ask me soon, they'll probably have to call an ambulance and take me away in a straitjacket, 'cause I'll have gone crazy from sheer curiosity."

"I guess I've been bumbling around, huh?" Darned if she didn't make him grin. He cleared his throat. "It was never that big a deal. I was just wondering...if you might come to dinner some time. Just once, you know? I was thinking that it might dispel some of the fascination you hold for Patrice, if she saw you at our place. Home. Plain old ordinary, normal surroundings." He added hastily, "It wouldn't be a date. Nothing like that. It would just be for Killer's sake. Not mine."

"Fine," Ariel said.

"Fine?"

Her eyebrows arched in delicate wings. "Did you think I'd give you a hard time? Sounds like a great idea to me. I'd be glad to. Just name the day and time."

But he couldn't right then, because someone in the bar called out his name. Ariel watched a short, mustached man with a growl of a laugh lope over to clap Josh on the shoulder. Josh made rushed introductions—the man's name was Sal Manelli, and evidently they'd grown up in the same neighborhood. She had her hand pumped, and Josh was teased over *finally* showing some good taste in women. His friend was a charmer with dark Italian eyes and a way of looking over a woman that made Ariel chuckle—he meant no harm; he was just full of nonsense.

Possibly Josh read the situation differently. Moving quickly, he reached in his back pocket for his wallet and slapped a bill on the table. Moving even quicker, he edged out of the booth and grabbed her hand. He never cut his old friend. He just put himself between Ariel and those sassy, dark Italian eyes. Sal was told regretfully that the last thing they wanted to do was leave.

But they sure seemed to be leaving fast, and Josh kept a handcuff grasp on her hand until they reached the door. Amused, Ariel glanced at his face. Did he really think she needed protecting from the big bad wolf? Sal was just...a guy. She'd been handling flirts since she was knee-high. Men were a comfortable part of her life.

Or they always had been, Ariel mused. How odd, that it had taken her twenty-nine years before she discovered there was one exception. Just one. After all this time.

The gentleman who opened the door for her with old-fashioned manners unquestionably threw her for six.

The silence was sudden when they walked outside. The smoky, noisy atmosphere of the bar disappeared as if another world opened when that door closed. It had turned dark. The sky cradled a silver crescent moon. The lights of the city shone above the rooftops like a dusty halo. The night was sleepy warm and magically hushed.

She wondered if Josh saw the magic.

She wondered if she'd ever met a man who was more uncomfortable around her.

She wondered if he knew how fiercely he pulled on her heart. There was so much love in him. Josh hadn't talked about anything but Patrice, but Ariel had heard more than the confusion of a struggling single dad. He put his family first—even if that meant doing something that made him personally uncomfortable. His asking her for dinner had come harder than pulling teeth, she mused, and he'd been so careful. Painstakingly careful to say that invitation was for Killer's sake. Not for his.

They crossed the parking lot in silence, until he abruptly stopped and hesitated. "I appreciate your coming," he said awkwardly.

"I was glad to. Thanks for the drink. And we got interrupted before you had the chance to tell me about dinner. You know—a day and time?"

"Oh...well, does Thursday night sound all right? Like around seven?"

"Sounds fine. You want me to bring anything?"

He didn't want her to bring anything. Ariel was pretty sure he wanted to back out of that invitation altogether, but he didn't know how. And she didn't offer him an out. He walked her to her car and said firmly, "I'll wait until you've got your keys."

That was apparently her cue to dig in her purse and come up with the little suckers. He wasn't about to leave a woman alone in a dark parking lot, she understood. But her purse was a crocheted bag, the kind where everything heaped in the black well of the bottom. It took a few minutes of fumbling before her fingers closed on the familiar crystal key chain.

Josh just stood there patiently, with his hands shoved in his front jeans pockets. She couldn't remember feeling more intensely aware of a man. The street lamp glowed on his dark hair, on the midnight shadows on his cheeks and chin. His shoulders were hunched, his collar as stiff as he was. His whole posture was tough, she thought fleetingly. Tough and lonely. She'd bet that the neighborhood moms hustled their daughters inside when he was a teenager, because he was the picture of what mothers worried about. A woman could get lost real quick in those dark magnetic eyes, and no female—at least no female—with a functioning heartbeat—could completely ignore the sexiness in the fit of his jeans, in the way he moved his hands, in the way he looked at a woman. Josh didn't seem to know. He didn't seem at all self-aware of being attractive, of being sexy, of being damn near irresistible.

"Are you having trouble finding your keys?" he asked.

"No. I've got them." Swiftly she raised the dangling key chain so he could see.

"Okay, then. Good night."

"Good night.... Josh?" He'd already half turned around when she called his name. He pivoted back on his heel, eyebrows raised in question, but she didn't really know why she'd impulsively called his name. She didn't have anything to say.

She didn't *know* she was going to reach up and touch his cheek. The gesture wasn't planned, wasn't thought out, wasn't even a floaty thought in her mind.

But he tensed like a poker. He suddenly wasn't moving, even to breathe. And his gaze suddenly scored on her face, seared on her mouth and face and eyes, as if he were freeze-framing her in his private VCR.

That was the first she knew that she was going to kiss him. Once that idea took root, it was harder to kill than a weed in a warm spring rain.

"Josh," she said gently, "I want you to know something. This is for your sake. Not for your daughter's. Not for your kids or anybody else's. This is just for you."

Five

If Josh had any idea what she was going to do, he'd have stopped her.

This is for your sake.... Just for you. Sure, he'd heard what she said. He just didn't have the first clue what she meant. And how could any ordinary male human being anticipate what a whirlwind was going to do?

When she touched his cheek, his hands were in his jeans pockets. Seconds before, that seemed like a handy place for his hands to be—not on her, not near her, but safe and sound out of temptation's way. Unfortunately, his hands were trapped in those snug pockets in the single millisecond when he might have avoided trouble. And then it was too late. The whirlwind had already tilted her head. And closed her eyes, so her lashes lay on her cheeks like pale velvet shadows. And then her mouth brushed his, rubbed alluringly against his, with lips softer than sunshine and sweeter than spring.

Aw, hell. He got his hands out of his pockets, but by then the blood was rushing through his veins and his heart was thudding like a hammer. He'd been a good guy, hadn't he? He'd been a gentleman. But he had a bad feeling—a sinking, trapped, worried feeling—that his Boy Scout good intentions just weren't going to last.

They'd kissed before, so Josh already knew how much potential trouble she was. Worse, he'd unwillingly begun to figure out that the rest of the world didn't necessarily see what he did. The guys in the bar, the bartender, Sal, all of them—they'd noticed her. A male would have to be deaf, dumb and blind not to notice her. But they'd treated her respectfully. There were always wolf whistles and catcalls when a good-looking woman walked in the bar. Not with her.

Somehow the others didn't see the come-hither touch to her smile, the sultry invitation in her eyes, the wild-and-willing body language. If nobody else was picking up the dangerous promises she was sending out, then possibly she was only transmitting to one mailbox. She was attracted to him. Not anybody else.

A terrifying thought.

The feel of her soft fingertips on his cheek was even more terrifying.

And her mouth...that silky-smooth tender mouth was the stuff of nightmares.

She wasn't for him. Josh understood that clearly. If she had a brain in her witless head, she should understand it clearly, too. Unlike him, she probably had a college degree. Surely that was a guarantee she had some smarts upstairs?

Maybe not. Slower than a sneaky breeze, her arms wound around his neck. That brought her closer. So close that her thighs grazed against his thighs, and the weight and warmth of her breasts crushed against his chest. Her hair floated, shimmering in the streetlight, and beneath that golden curtain his hands unwillingly, foolishly, stupidly molded down her spine and snugged her tight to him.

He was aroused. Hell, he'd been rock hard even before his tongue stole inside her mouth and intimately sampled his first peach daiquiri. It was sweet, but not nearly as sweet or heady as the taste of her. Okay, he thought. Okay. I'm not addicted. I'm just trying this drug once. It wasn't as if he'd die if he couldn't have it.

But it felt that way. As if he might just blow apart if he had to let her go. Nobody kissed him like she did—not Nancy, not the women before his ex-wife, not all the girls who'd been part of his teenage years. Ariel took him back to those times. He remembered when his hormones had been on a constant collision course with disaster. He remembered loving it. He remembered when sex was all about anticipation and wonder and the blind-crazy feeling that nothing was better, nothing, than kissing his girl and half dying from the forbidden richness of wanting.

She murmured something against his lips. A soft cry, a call, with his name labeled in her fierce, throaty whisper. He took her mouth again, dipping deeper this time. It wasn't real. Reality was his kids, his work, his messy divorce and a life he was racing hard to keep up with. It had nothing to do with peach-daiquiri-flavored kisses and a woman coming on to him, tempting him beyond all reason with her beguiling soft kisses and wild, yielding responsiveness.

This couldn't be happening to him. Josh had no problem reaching that easy, logical, comforting conclusion. His body just couldn't seem to catch up with that practical message.

The scarf at her neck fluttered to the ground, baring her long white throat, and her whole body arched when his mouth embedded kisses down the length, in the hollows, on the pulse point. Her heart was beating hard now, but not half as thundering-loud as his. Beneath her blouse, her skin warmed under the rubbing caress of his hands. Against his shirt, against his heartbeat, he could feel her nipples tightening and her breasts turning achingly firm.

He didn't believe she belonged to him, yet his pulse sang low and hot to just that tune. She responded with such fire and longing. She responded as if she knew him as a lover, desired him as a lover, and he wanted to see her bare. He wanted to touch her bare. He wanted her beneath him, naked, on a hard mattress behind a locked door. He'd wash her down with feather kisses. He'd take her good, good and hard and high, so high that she'd cry out with the sheer power and exhaustion of that damn much pleasure.

A wolf whistle echoed in the night, followed by the low burst of masculine teasing laughter.

Josh's head shot up. So did hers.

A group of guys from the bar were headed for their cars, old construction buddies, who shot him some tribal winks and locker room gestures in appreciation of the ringside show. Swiftly Josh pressed her cheek into his shoulder, instinctively wanting to shield her face from their eyes. What was it about a couple of beers that turned grown men into eternal adolescents? But even the shock of a sudden interruption failed to slow down his galloping pulse. His whole body was still tight and hard from frustrated desire.

Car doors slammed and engines fired. Within seconds, they were alone again. And within seconds, Ariel had lifted her head. She was smiling.

God knew why. One glance at her face, and guilt roiled through him. Holy kamoly, he'd half destroyed her. A cloisonné comb was hanging cockeyed from her hair. Her silk scarf—the thing probably cost a fortune—lay in an abandoned heap on the asphalt. So did her purse and car keys. The shimmery blouse was no longer neatly tucked into her denim skirt, but bunched with one tail free and the neckline all askew. Her eyes had the sleepy, shy look of a dreamer's, and her mouth no longer had lipstick. Her lips were rough red and swollen, vulnerably swollen from the pressure of his kisses, and damned if that beguiling, bedeviling smile didn't make him want to kiss her all over again.

He bent down and scooped up her scarf and purse instead. Sober as a judge—he couldn't have touched his mother with more respect—he tried to tie the scarf around her neck. It seemed a good idea, a downright outstanding idea, to cover that tempting long white throat. And since he was the one who'd messed her up, he felt responsible for putting her back together. Only, handling a moving snake had to be easier than managing that scarf. The material slipped and slid. He remembered how she wore the thing, tied real casually, real carelessly, real artsy and cute and all, only he couldn't make it look anything better than an uneven, drunken noose.

She made a sound, something like a chortling laugh, that made him glance at her. She pointed with a finger to her neck.

Well, hell. He was *trying* to fix her. Not choke her to death. Face flushed and fingers fumbling, he loosened the knot.

"Better," she murmured with another laugh.

"I...um..." So far he hadn't managed to say anything. He needed, really needed, to come up with something better than "I...um," but his brain was operating on mush power. He dropped his hands.

So did she. "It's okay," she said gently, which was about the silliest thing he'd ever heard. She wasn't okay. He wasn't okay. Nothing he'd done to her in the past half hour was remotely okay. Why couldn't life come with a handy erase button he could push for awkward, embarrassing moments like this?

He managed to make sure she had her keys and her purse, watched her climb in her car and start that purr of an engine. But he didn't scalp a hand through his hair—didn't even try to breathe—until the shiny red tail of her Midget had turned out of the parking lot.

A loud sigh hissed out of his lungs then. Damned if he knew what he was feeling. Anxiety? Frustration? Confusion? Or an emotional rats' nest of all three. If the guys hadn't interrupted them, Josh wasn't positive where that embrace would have ended up. He'd been lost, swimming-blind lost. In her. How it happened at all confounded him. He never had, never would, believe in magic, but she sure as hell did something to bewitch him.

Josh considered himself an ordinary, average guy with an ordinary average dose of healthy hormones. But he'd never been sabotaged by his glands before.

No matter what the provocation, a man stuck to his values. A good man tried to live his life so he didn't have to make apologies. And a thirty-four-year-old man who'd traveled some experienced life roads knew better than to bite into Eve's apple.

Ariel was forbidden fruit. Tempting to taste in a fantasy, but no way, nohow, could she fit in his life. Just like his daughter, Josh thought glumly, she was a stealer and a thief. Only, in Ariel's case, they were talking a stealer of hearts. A thief of a man's sanity.

Impatiently he dug in his pocket for his truck keys.

Sanity was returning now, thankfully fast and reassuringly familiar. For every problem, there was a pragmatic solution. He hadn't forgotten about asking her for dinner on Thursday. Seeing her again would be awkward, but that was irrelevant. It would give her a chance to see his place, his family, how they really lived, who he really was.

If she was harboring any terrifyingly unnerving ideas about being attracted to him, dinner should resolve that issue real quickly.

A man...well, a man just wasn't like a woman. Women tended to respond to things emotionally. Men didn't let that happen. No man worth his testosterone ran away from a problem. He took control.

Ariel could smell burned spaghetti from halfway down the block.

She paid no attention at first. The vague smell came from a distance and hardly rated as a fascinating distraction—everyone had burned a dinner sometime. The houses were packed too close together on the tree-lined street to identify which one the fumes were emanating from, assuming she cared—which she didn't.

Her thoughts were already a confused tangle over the coming evening. Josh and his family were the only things on her mind.

She'd chosen to walk to his place, rather than drive. The exercise, she hoped, would help soothe the bouncing butterflies in her stomach. And that was working, until she reached the meandering bend in the hillside cul-de-sac that led to Josh's house.

It wasn't seven yet. Hazy sunlight filtered through the maples and birch trees. A silky, balmy breeze barely stirred the leaves. It was an old neighborhood, chock-full of character. Above her head, the overgrown maples looked like dancers' green cancan skirts, and her sandals made clicking sounds on the worn, cracked pavement. Children screamed as they raced through an ice-cold sprinkler. Cats snoozed on porches. Nobody who lived on Valley Road was rich, but shutters were freshly painted, petunias and marigolds thrived in flower beds, porch steps looked just-swept.

There was only one exception. Ariel didn't need to read the mailbox number to identify Josh's house. The look of his place made an unsettling lump lodge in her throat.

The white frame, peaked-roof bungalow with the forest-green shutters wasn't shouting-different from the other houses. She'd half expected to see the basketball hoop nailed over the garage, and the ragtag set of bikes in the driveway—including the one with training wheels—was no surprise.

But there were no chairs on his front porch, no flowers in the barren beds, and her gaze was inevitably drawn to the white draperies hanging from the front picture window. They were the pinch-pleat type of drapes that took a traverse rod, obvious because of the saggy droop in the curtain—obviously a hook or two had been lost. Ariel was unsure why that small, saggy droop struck her as so...lonely. Nothing else about the house or fresh-mowed yard looked neglected.

It was just that the house so blatantly lacked any woman's influence. Anyone could tell it was a home without a mom. A home that was noticeably missing a wife.

Her fingers itched to fix those stupid curtain hooks—a startling and silly impulse, considering that she'd draped bed sheets over a couple of nails for her own window decor. She'd never been the domesticated type. Never worried about it. The role of a wife had never been on her goal list. From the time she'd graduated from diapers, she'd watched everyone in her life rollercoaster down the marriage track to heartbreak. She wasn't knocking the institution. She just personally wanted no part of it.

Knowing Josh hadn't changed her mind.

Being with him, though, confused her. She thought they'd been honest with each other. His divorce was recent. If and when he started looking again, Ariel had no doubt he'd search for the kind of woman who was seriously potential mom and wife material. She'd been frank—that wasn't her. Chalk and cheese made an unpalatable sandwich. That wasn't hard to figure out. Yet they'd only been alone together twice, and both times, magic had exploded between them like a witch's unpredictable brew. Where that wild, abandoned embrace in the parking lot came from, she still had no idea, but Josh, damn him, had taken her out. The power of emotion between them had made her feel wondrous and shaky and intoxicated...and scared.

She shouldn't be feeling that way for a man she couldn't have. She shouldn't be wanting to fix his silly curtain hooks. She shouldn't be experiencing a fierce, clenching feeling of belonging to a man who, for cripes' sake, very possibly didn't even like her.

You're only here for Patrice, Ariel reminded herself, and immediately calmed down. It really was true. This whole dinner had nothing to do with Josh. She was only here because of the Kleptomaniac Kid. Somehow Patrice had developed an unhealthy fascination with her, and never mind that the urchin had stolen her heart. Ariel could surely help the little one. She'd dressed in cutoffs, T-shirt and sandals, playclothes to wear around kids, clothes to show Killer that she was as ordinary as chicken soup.

Her step picked up a spring as she headed up the drive. She could do this. Help the urchin—and steer clear of the little one's dad—if she just kept her priorities straight.

Her priorities were crystal-clear and rod-straight as she bounced up the porch steps. The smell of burned spaghetti suddenly hit her again. This time it was stronger. This time...malodorous.

Good Lord, it stank.

With a frown, she reached to knock on the screen door...and then abruptly changed her mind about knocking. She caught the drift of smoke in the silky breeze. And from inside the house, she heard the sounds of shouting and pounding footsteps, and then suddenly, the ear-shattering screech of a smoke alarm.

"Holy kamoly, what the hell happened around here! Bruiser, get that window and door open...

Calvin, get on a chair and turn that confounded thing off. Patrice, would you quit crying! Dammit, there's nothing to be scared of! Bruiser, get your sister out of harm's way. Yeeeouch! Get *away* from the stove, all of you! Where the hell are the hot pads?''

Ariel hit the hall at a dead run, tripping over a mountainous-size pair of basketball shoes and pushing aside a doll carriage en route. She passed a brown-and-white living room with a TV and stereo blaring simultaneously, then a peach bathroom that smelled of lime shaving cream and the humid steam from a recent shower. She sprinted faster. The unfamiliar layout of the house presented no problem. Josh let loose a string of four-letter words loud enough to make tracking him down easy.

She only paused for three seconds in the kitchen doorway—long enough to take in the pandemonium. Killer was standing on a kitchen chair, screaming and crying. The smoke alarm was screeching at top volume, Calvin scrambling to stand on top of the table where he could reach it. A hodgepodge of mismatched dishes and cutlery had been meticulously, neatly set at the table—at least until Calvin tried to walk around the china with his oversize Nike sneakers. A salad bowl teetered. A plate crashed. Worse, flames were shooting from a stove burner, wrapping around a Dutch oven filled with bubbling spaghetti.

Really bubbling. Spaghetti sauce was spurting in minivolcano geysers all over the place, including on Josh, who looked as if he'd just climbed out of a shower—his hair was wet, his jeans unbuttoned, his right cheek still slathered white with shaving cream. His chest was bare, tautly muscled and golden skinned, smooth except for a springy pattern of dark hair arching down his rib cage. Another time, Ariel might have given that naked virile chest another look. But just then his whole torso was polka-dotting fast with hot spaghetti sauce—*burning* hot spaghetti sauce, judging from the descriptive language he was using.

There just wasn't time to say hi.

She spotted the Dutch oven lid on the far white Formica counter and jogged for it. Once she slammed the lid on the pot, the sauce quit spurting. At the same instant, Josh flicked off the burner. Bruiser showed up with a fire extinguisher, and dropped that at his father's shout to open the back door. Calvin disconnected the smoke alarm at the same time Josh grabbed the blackened pot with hot pads and sprinted out the back door with it. The stovetop flames sizzled down to sparks, then died.

Faster than a finger snap, total chaos turned to total quiet, but everyone seemed to be out of breath, including Ariel. Josh showed up back in the doorway, but he just leaned there for a second. Bruiser was helpfully waving smoke out the open window. Calvin slowly climbed down from the table. The kitchen had been blue-and-white once. Now, streaks of spaghetti sauce decorated the floor, the ceiling, the walls and for sure every counter space for a mile around the stove.

They all knew she was there—they'd seen her running around along with the rest of them—but no one had a chance to say anything yet. Killer recovered first. The urchin was still standing on a kitchen chair, one arm wrapped around an obviously well-loved and well-worn stuffed animal. Her tearstained face abruptly wreathed in a smile.

"Hi, Ariel," she said.

"Hi, Ariel," Bruiser echoed.

Josh closed his eyes and clawed a hand through his hair. "Hi, Ariel," he said, his tone drier than the Sahara. "Welcome to dinner at the Penoyer house."

"That," Calvin confided to her, "was my dad's foolproof spaghetti."

Six

_____

Bruiser shot to the left and tossed Ariel the basketball. She dribbled it twice, then streaked under Josh's arm and leapt in the air. The basketball smacked against the backboard and then went through the net, clean as a baby. Bruiser and Ariel chortled with glee, exuberantly sharing a clapping-loud high-five. It wasn't the first time.

"Dad," Calvin said disgustedly, "we're getting creamed."

Josh knew. But how was he supposed to guess that that bit of a woman knew how to shoot round ball, much less that she played basketball for blood?

"Daddy, aren't you guys through playing yet?" Killer complained loudly from the sidelines.

"Five minutes more, squirt. That's all. I promise." They'd started playing at dusk. It was now full dark, pitch-dark except for yard lights and a witch's half-moon, but Josh had the ball. His masculine prowess was on the line. So was saving face in front of his sons. He'd keep to that promise of five minutes, but damn, he wanted to score.

He dribbled, facing his guard, using eye-contact intimidation to distract her. He faked a feint to the right. She wasn't fooled. He glanced at Calvin—a clear signal any guy would understand to mean he intended to pass the ball—but she wasn't fooled by that, either.

This close, he could see the bloodthirsty gleam in her eyes. This close, he could see the fluorescent green T-shirt clinging damply to her breasts, the pearl shine on her cheeks. Before the game, she'd scraped her hair up with a rubber band. Silvery gold strands were poking out all over the place now, framing a face that was tense, eyes chock-full of violence and passionate concentration. With her bent over, he could see the way those skimpy cutoffs hugged her butt—about as perfect and sexy a behind as he'd ever seen on a woman— but this time, no way this time, was he gonna be distracted.

He dribbled in, rushing her. Her arms shot up to block his shot of the ball. His aim was true. In fact, his aim was perfect. It was just for the eeniest millisecond, when her arms raised above her head, that his gaze dropped to the firm, ripe protrusion of her nipples beneath that damned T-shirt.

The basketball flew through the air, teetered on the rim of the net and then fell—no score—to the ground.

"Dad, you shoulda been able to make that in your sleep," Calvin said despairingly.

Bruiser made a ridiculous attempt to sound consoling. "Hey, don't blame Dad for being outplayed. It's not *his* fault we're better than you guys, is it, Ariel?"

Josh exchanged glances with his oldest as the opposing team pranced around the driveway, slapping hands and lording it up about their victory with a shameless lack of mercy.

"Does this mean you guys are *finally* through?" Patrice wailed plaintively.

"It sure does," Ariel said joyfully, and swooped down on the little girl. "I believe I promised you a story before bed. Maybe even two."

"I thought you forgot me," Patrice said woefully.

"Are you kidding me? In this lifetime, I'd never forget you. Did you pick out a special book for me to read?"

Within minutes the clan had dispersed. Ariel and Patrice disappeared upstairs with an armload of books, Bruiser grabbed the telephone and Calvin switched on his computer.

Josh ambled into the kitchen, opened the fridge and cracked the lid on a beer. One long gulp satisfied his parched throat, but it didn't solve his sudden problem with restlessness. He glanced around the kitchen. Although the god-awful spaghetti mess had been cleaned up, the smoky smell still lingered.

Nothing about this evening had gone as planned. Not one cotton-picking thing.

He yanked on a sweatshirt and then headed outside, flicking off the glaring porch light before settling on the front steps with his beer. The temperature was dropping fast now. It was cool outside. Cool, quiet and blessedly dark.

He stretched out his legs, thinking that he didn't really mind about the disastrous dinner. In fact—if he'd had a brain—he'd have planned the disaster ahead of time. He'd never wanted to impress Ariel or put on the dog. The burned spaghetti was a brilliant, telling example of how life was around his house. Constant chaos. Nothing you could predict from one minute to the next. Messes, yelling, tempers, swearing and confusion. It should have scared Ariel off him and his family real easy.

Only, it hadn't worked out that way.

He rolled his shoulders, staring at the fireflies dancing in the yard. His kids had been all over her like ants on honey. She'd been a trooper about cleaning up the mess, had his whole group laughing and chipping in.

She'd taken him on, too. Feeling embarrassed that she'd found him half-dressed with a face half-streaked with shaving cream—and in such a mess—did no good. He'd had a couple of stinging burns from the blasted spaghetti, spots on his bare chest that stung like fire and a real streak of a burn on his left hand.

Ariel had had his palm under cold running tap water before he could even swear, then had nosed around his cupboards and ferreted out the first-aid supplies without being asked. He could take care of himself, for Pete's sake. But she'd applied the salve, her fingertips gentle, careful, sure . . . and erotic as hell.

Disturbingly erotic. Alluringly erotic. Particularly when it was out of line—way, way, way out of line—to be even thinking about sex in front of his kids.

He set down his beer and leaned back on his elbows. She'd done exactly what he wanted. Except for that little incident with the salve, she hadn't paid him a lick of personal attention. No shy looks his way. No come-hither smiles. No hint that that intimate embrace the other night had ever happened. They'd had take-out tacos on the picnic table in the backyard, played a little round ball. She'd taken care not to flourish any special attention on Killer, treating her no differently than the boys, just being easy and casual and fun, acting like an adult friend, nothing more.

She'd done just right, only, it was like one of those stories in which the surgery was successful but the patient died.

His kids were enchanted with her.

And getting more enchanted.

It worried him—worried him like the nag of a mosquito—that his brood had already cast her in the role of potential mom. It disturbed him far more that Ariel fit in as if she had a gut-blood tie to the family... when she was a woman who didn't believe in families.

He heard the creak of footsteps from the stairs, then her lilting voice chitchatting with the boys. Every muscle in his shoulder was braced even before he heard the squeak of the screen door.

"I was wondering where you were. Patrice fell asleep while we were reading, Josh. I tucked her in."

"I thought she might drop off. Pretty late bedtime for the squirt." He lurched to his feet, careful to keep his eyes off her. Even so, he noticed she'd brushed out all the tangles from her hair, and it was hanging loose, the color of moonlight, in a swinging sweep down her back. "You're probably beat. We didn't exactly give you a restful evening around here, did we?"

"Maybe not exactly restful. But I had fun." There was a smile in her voice. A smile as smoky as that moonlight.

"If you're ready to go, I'll walk you home," he said abruptly.

"Heavens, you don't have to do that. It's only a few blocks, and I would have driven if I'd been worried about walking home alone."

She was right about the distance, but those "few blocks" included a cut through a dark, woody ravine and then a stroll down the back alley behind her store. She was walking home alone the same day it snowed in Mexico, but Josh suspected he wouldn't get too far if he put it in those terms. A fib would get the same job done. "I could use an excuse to stretch my legs. Just give me a second to tell the boys where I'm going," he said.

He went back in, told the boys, and on his jog back through the hall grabbed a jacket. Not for him. His black sweatshirt was ample protection against the cooling night, but she was only wearing a thin T-shirt over those ragged cutoffs.

Once outside, he dropped the jacket on her shoulders. "Thanks," she murmured in surprise, and snuggled into the warmth. "I didn't realize it was going to get this chilly."

She should have. Connecticut summer nights always cooled down. She looked pretty silly in his old aviator jacket with the too-long sleeves, but at least it covered that wicked T-shirt. The slogan on the front had first caught his eye for its shock effect. It read I'd Do Anything For Tall, Dark and Rich, leading anybody to assume certain things about her taste in men. They'd been halfway through dinner before she happened to turn around and he caught the single word on the backside of the shirt— Chocolate.

Josh had seen the humor. By then, though, it was a little late. Through the whole evening, his gaze had strayed to the printed Rich on that shirt. The *ic* in the word dipped in the spoon of her cleavage. Her nipples poked out of the *r* and *h*. It was a bad word, *rich*. A dangerous word. A word he avoided, the same way he steered clear of other things he couldn't have. No point obsessing on dreams that were way, way out of his ken.

She was covered now, though. And once she flipped her hair out from behind the collar, she smiled at him again, and then charged down the walk. A fast pace suited him fine. So would silence, but he wasn't that lucky.

"Josh?" She hesitated. "I'm not sure we accomplished what we wanted with the dinner."

"I'm not, either."

"It's pretty hard to ignore—how hungry your kids are for a mom. I don't really think it has anything to do with me. I'd guess any woman you brought around would get the same checkout, the same shy little hints. Especially from your youngest." She shot him a wry glance. "Killer came right out and asked me if I was going to marry you. My stomach must have dropped ten feet. I told her no way, José, that I was just a friend to you, no different than I'm friends with her, and that marriage wasn't even a remote possibility— not for me—and that you already knew that."

Josh pushed his hands in his pockets. The kids had mortified him half to death with their bulldozer-subtle matchmaking hints, but he'd had no idea Killer had taken it so far. His tone was gruff with awkwardness. "I'm sorry my monster put you through that."

"Don't be. I'm not. Kids have a habit of asking honest questions. They don't mean to be embarrassing. And maybe it helped. It seemed to be a brand-new idea for her—that you could have a woman friend without the whole marriage ball of wax being part of the picture."

A squirrel darted across the sidewalk in front of them. Lights switched off at the O'Learys' house, then the Krackovs'. His neighborhood was going to bed. Leaves rustled in the sudden fretful breeze, a lonely night wind that stirred strange, uneasy feelings.

It struck him as bafflingly ironic that she was the one woman he could talk to about this—and the only woman he felt safe bringing home. God knew what matchmaking nonsense the kids might pull on someone else, but Ariel had handled the situation better than he could. Who would ever guess that they'd be reading from the same page? Yet he really wasn't worried about his kids getting hurt or building up unrealistic expectations around her, because the confounded woman was more dead set against marriage than he could ever be.

They crossed the empty lot toward the wooded ravine. Pale lights twinkled through the heavy umbrella of leaves. The path was strewn with twigs and pinecones—hard walking with her in sandals—but the back alley to her store and apartment was just on the other side. "Pretty hard to believe you're not going to change your mind about marriage sometime."

She chuckled. "I'm twenty-nine. And it hasn't happened yet."

He pushed aside a branch before it could slap her. "Yeah, well, maybe you haven't been in love yet."

She really laughed then, a soft sound in the darkness. "I've been in love often. I *love* being in love—who doesn't? I just got smart enough to realize that the first blush on the rose never lasts."

Talking to her was like opening a book he couldn't put down. It wasn't his business what she thought or believed, but he couldn't reconcile the cynic with the believer in magic—not without at least trying to understand. "The blush on the rose isn't supposed to last. Nature hooks you on chemistry. That's the way it's supposed to be. After that, well...you never heard of the word *commitment?*"

"I hear people talking about it. I don't see anyone doing it. And at this point in time, I'm not sure it matters. A woman doesn't need a man to support her anymore. And no one says boo if a woman chooses to have a child alone. Mason used to tell me I had a harder head than a bulldog on the subject, but frankly I think I'm being a realist. Putting a wedding ring on your finger doesn't seem to have anything to do with commitment—"

"Who's Mason?"

At the top of the ravine, they startled a raccoon, who stared at them with bandit's eyes before waddling off. "Mason's an old friend. He's an English prof, teaches in Boston now. I lived with him for almost three years—"

"You lived with this guy?"

She glanced at him. Her tone turned droll and dry. "I may be antimarriage, but that doesn't mean I plan to be celibate for the rest of my life. And Mason wasn't the first man I loved. There was a guy in college. George. And after George, I fell harder than lead for a man named Bryan. They were all terrific guys. In fact, I still keep in touch with all of them.''

''You stayed friends with all those guys?''

''Sure. You find that odd?'' Her brows feathered in soft wings. ''I was always honest with anyone I've been involved with, as far as my feelings about marriage and ties. When the relationship was over, it was over. But we always parted on friendly terms.''

Not him. Even before Nancy, when Josh broke with a woman, the ending was inevitably stormy. He'd never played the game halfway. When a man loved hard, he fought with the same kind of passion. Why bother with a relationship when the emotion wasn't volatile and strong?

Josh wouldn't have minded five minutes alone with that guy Mason. And it gnawed on him. On the surface, Ariel touted a real wild, uncommitted, free-love type of life-style. Immoral, on his terms.

But it wasn't ''immoral'' he heard. It was vulnerability. Stubborn, block-headed, lonely, defensive vulnerability. She wasn't going to risk traveling the same road as her parents. Her mind was as set as a rock. Nobody was gonna convince her that it didn't have to be that way.

Odd, how he had to clamp his jaw shut to keep from arguing with her. He was coming from the scars of his own failed marriage, making any argument he could try beyond humorous. Still, she was a fresh-born baby as far as he could see, a virgin emotionally, no matter how many damn wimps had conned their way into her bed. Josh would spit nails before admitting it in a mens' locker room, but free sex was worth dandelions, an easy lay inevitably boring as hell. The passion that came from knowing someone, really knowing, really trusting, was part of the lottery a man and woman won together.

Shut up, Penoyer. And he obeyed that warning scolding in his mind. If Ariel wanted to sleep with a hundred men, it was none of his business. If she couldn't see that she was vulnerable as hell, laying herself bare to be taken for a ride by the real scoundrels in life—hey, she was an adult.

And they were doing fine, he thought, as they crossed the alley to her back stairs. Just fine. Essentially the whole conversation had helped clear up some sticky air. Maybe their values were polar opposites, but discovering that was a relief. She couldn't want to be involved with him, any more than he wanted to be tempted by her. That was settled. He was sure.

He cleared his throat at the top of the stairs. "You were good with my kids."

Her eyes flashed to his, warm with honesty. "I wouldn't hurt them."

He nodded. "I wasn't sure how it was going to go, my asking you to dinner. But I think what you said was right. It was good for the kids to see us behaving like friends, nothing more."

"Well, at least it put the idea in their heads that you can be just friends with a woman," she agreed, and then hesitated. "I like your kids. I'd like to be a friend if they need one, and Patrice...I'd feel badly if you forbid her from coming around the shop. I really love her, Josh."

"Yeah, I love her, too. And I won't forbid her from coming around, as long as she's not being a pest."

"I'll watch her real carefully if she stops in," Ariel promised.

He swiped a hand over his face. "Here's hoping your coming to dinner put paid to that little klepto-maniac streak she was running."

She grinned. "I never thought that was going to last long, but if you think it would help, we could get to-gether again sometime. Just casually. Maybe it would help engrain the idea that you can have a woman friend who's not . . . well . . . a romantic interest."

"Yeah. Good idea."

And that was that for the evening, Ariel thought. She lifted up and dug the apartment key from the pocket of her white cutoffs. On an afterthought, she remembered she was wearing his jacket and peeled it off. Josh hooked it over his shoulder, but he didn't budge until she turned the key and pushed the back door open, and even then he protectively glanced around. There was no one in the alley, though, no cars, no bodies, just the restlessly moving shadows of trees being tossed by a moonlit wind.

"Well, good night," he said abruptly, "and thanks again."

"'Night."

He'd climbed three steps down when he suddenly pivoted around. Ariel saw him turn. She smiled an-other good-night. She was still smiling when he bounded back up the metal stairs.

They'd agreed, she thought, to be friends. Josh wasn't a subtle man. His expression X-rayed his thoughts and opinions as clearly as his blunt conver-sation. His kids were vulnerable, his feelings for any woman were inseparable from those kids, and staying no more than platonic friends was safest for every-one.

His mouth latched onto hers like the fit of a pin in a grenade. What the Sam Hill happened to *safe?* Lord. She'd already opened the door with her key, but now it banged back, her spine layered flat with the power of that kiss. The shadows in her tiny vestibule were blacker than tar, but she could still see his face. The fire in his eyes was darker, wilder, than an unpredictable summer storm, black lightning that seemed to come from nowhere.

All night, she'd wanted to touch him. All night, she'd felt the sizzle and simmer of electricity between them. All night, she'd come to accept and understand he didn't want this. He didn't want her. His kids came first with him; with Josh, that meant taking no risks where they were concerned, and she fiercely, sincerely agreed that she'd never do anything that could hurt his kids, either. That was all real.

But the man coming apart in her arms was real, too. His tongue sought hers. Took hers. His hands wrapped in her hair, tugging her to him, his face angled to deepen a kiss that was already dipping in deep, dark waters. Dangerous waters. Her blood rushed. Desire knotted in her stomach, then knotted tighter.

The drumbeat in her ears roared, blocking out the rumble of the furnace, the cheerful beat of the kitchen clock in some other universe. A foolish phone was ringing somewhere. She paid no attention; Josh didn't even seem to hear it, and eventually it had the good sense to quit.

She told herself he was scaring her, he was so rough, but that wasn't really true. Maybe she had no idea what blew the lid off, but no one was always tough. No one was always strong. No one could stash needs and feelings in a closet forever, no matter how hard he'd been trying. She wasn't afraid, but she was shaken... and getting shakier.

One kiss spun into another, then spiraled into another and another. He'd be no Harvard lover. The thought made her heartbeat skitter and race. There'd be no pleases and thank-yous and psychobabble discussion about relationships. He made the other men she'd known seem wonderfully, safely civilized. Josh, she sensed, would never be so reasonable. Passion was elemental for him. If he took her, it'd be the most primitive kind of claim.

That was how he made her feel. As if he were claiming the taste and texture of her mouth like a bandit on a lawless rampage. Her breasts firmed, ached, hurt when he cupped her, his palm ignoring the T-shirt as if the cloth didn't exist, his thumb brushing her nipples until they stood up for his attention. Shameless. Her whole body was responding to him shamelessly, like it was him, only him, that every nerve ending had been waiting for since the day she was born.

Her fingers clenched, then unclenched, as they traveled up his arms and wrapped around his neck. She didn't exactly mean to invite more trouble. It was just that her knees were turning into water, and his loneliness, the fierce wild longing she sensed in his touch, was something she had to respond to. She believed in magic, always had, found evidence of magic everywhere in life. But not this kind. Not this raw, real kind of excitement that wrapped around the magic in her soul. *I know you, Josh. I've known you my whole life. I just never met you before....*

His denim jeans scratched abrasively against her bare thighs, but she could feel his arousal pressed between them. She could feel the heat, feel his size, feel his palms moving down her spine now, moving down to cup her fanny and mold her tight and hard against him. No fire had ever been this hot. No storm had ever been this wild. And confusing her completely was the texture of silk.

His mouth kept rubbing against hers like warm, wet silk, a hunger in him that her most willing kisses couldn't seem to appease. She didn't know when his touch had gentled. She didn't know when all that lawless roughness disappeared and this fierce softness took its place. Right then, she didn't know her own name.

He lifted his head suddenly. He was breathing hard, hoarse and low, and his eyes looked dazed. They lanced on her face, as if she were a compass and he'd never been this lost. He took a long breath. His hand unsteadily reached up. A rough callused thumb traced the seam of her lips.

He whispered, "Dammit, Ariel," but it sounded like a caress.

He took another breath. "I didn't mean that to happen, didn't plan it to happen."

She found her voice, although it seemed to be coming from the distance to Atlanta. "I never thought you did."

A thundercloud of an exasperated frown bunched his brows together. "You want to hit me?"

"No."

"I'd feel better if you did. Believe me, I'd understand. If I were in *your* shoes, I'd sock me." He stepped back, as if giving her ample space to take advantage of that option. When she did nothing, he scalped a hand through his hair. "Damnation. I don't understand why this keeps happening."

It was like trying to soothe a wounded beast. "Because you're human? And maybe have some needs and feelings that won't stay buttonholed just because you want them to?"

His eyes locked on hers. "No. I had no problem keeping a buttonhole on control before. Until you. Something keeps happening when the two of us are together, and I don't understand it."

"You're blaming me?" she asked quietly.

"Blame?" He touched her cheek again. "Honey, you're not getting this. I'm not mad at you. I'm mad at *me*. I'm sorry for jumping you, sorry for taking advantage. I was way out of line, and I swear, it won't happen again."

Seven

"So he scalps them when they're still alive. The cops realize it's the same m.o. because they've come across the results of the slaughter five times now—but they don't know *why*. He only preys on young women with long hair—they're always naked and they're always scalped—"

"Gruesome," Ariel murmured politely. She touched the brownies. They were nicely bubbled on top, and still warm from the oven—but not so hot they couldn't be served.

She opened the cutlery drawer for a knife, sparing an absent glance at her friend. Actually, Jeanne was more adopted family than just a pal—which was why Ariel had gone to the trouble of dragging, bribing and bullying her into coming for dinner.

No stranger, looking at Jeanne, would ever guess she was a successful writer. Her short blond hair stuck

up in cowlicks, her socks didn't match and a pair of
ancient sweatpants bagged on her slight, skinny frame.
Whenever she was midway through writing a book,
she looked like an orphaned derelict, and God knew
she'd forget to eat if Ariel didn't occasionally step in
and take charge.

"The woman has to be beautiful," Jeanne contin-
ued. "Like his sister. Because of what his sister did to
him when they were kids—"

"Hmm," Ariel murmured encouragingly. Nothing
more than ums and hmms were ever required from
these conversations. There was no way her shy, gentle
friend was going to be diverted from anything but
blood, guts and torture.

After slicing the brownies into huge squares, she
raided the fridge for ice cream and maraschino cherries, then generously scooped a double mound of ice
cream on both treats. Jeanne needed fattening up.
Ariel just wanted the solace of a familiar comfort
food.

"So his next intended victim, of course, is the her-
oine. She's already running away from an abusive
husband, so she's alone and vulnerable."

"Hmm." Ariel put the plate in her friend's hand,
then herded her into the living room, where both settled Indian-style on the carpet by the coffee table. Her
mind was on Josh. Nothing new. Her thoughts had
been snarled and tangled on Mr. Joshua Penoyer for
the past three days. She'd blown men out of her mind
before, though, and she could do it again.

She popped a cherry into her mouth. Her teeth
scrunched down on the succulent sweet taste. It was
meltingly good, sinfully, irresistibly good. Almost as
good as sex.

Sex, she thought darkly, was the problem. Pheromones, hormones and all that other blasted chemistry. Josh desired her. It wasn't tough to figure that out. But his response to her was chemical rather than emotional—he didn't *want* to want her. And she didn't mess with men who were going to cause her heartache.

She shoveled in a mouthful of brownie.

The man had scared her. She wasn't ashamed to admit it. There were men she could handle and men she couldn't. Josh was a "couldn't." Damned if she knew what had happened three nights ago, but it wasn't funny, that overwhelming feeling of longing and belonging. It wasn't cute, knowing she'd felt so immersed in That Man that he could have taken her standing up, against the back door, and she'd never have said more than "Please." He'd made her feel as if he were her soul mate, as if she'd finally found the one man who reached her, touched her, understood her at some deep feminine soul level.

Poppycock.

There'd been nothing wrong with her life. She'd been content—perfectly, wonderfully content—until Josh had popped into her life and started causing these alien, unfamiliar, unsettling emotions. Somehow he had her thinking about impossible words such as *mom,* mulling silly and archaic words such as *wife.*

Only a lunatic believed that a leopard could really change her spots. *And that's it, Penoyer. I'm gonna stay far, far away from you. You've shaken me up for the last time. I'm not going to think about you anymore. I'm not going to waste another single thought on you....*

"So...he goes at her with a spear. Aiming for the artery in her throat..." Jeanne was still thinking aloud, still lost in her plot, and forking down a second brownie when she suddenly looked up. "What's that?"

"What's what?"

"I think someone's knocking at your back door."

Ariel listened, then finally caught the faint, muffled rhythmic thud. She pushed her plate onto the coffee table and padded barefoot to the back door.

When she opened it, an invisible band tightened around her temples—and maybe her heart, too. Bare milliseconds before, she'd sworn off thinking about Josh. And she'd meant it. She'd just temporarily forgotten that there were other members of the Penoyer clan who tugged on her heart with no less mercy than Josh.

Killer was balancing on one foot, a baseball cap perched backward and askew over her cockeyed braids, a huge fistful of grubby, wilted wildflowers wrapped in one hand. "Hi, Ariel." That hopelessly plain face peered up at her with eyes chock-full of anticipation. "These are from my dad. For you."

Ariel took the thrust-out flowers before they fell. "I...um...thank you. From your dad, huh?" The chances of Josh picking those sad-looking wildflowers were about a zillion to one. But the urchin met her eyes squarely. She had a limitless career ahead of her as a politician, Ariel thought, if she could lie that well.

"Dad had to work late tonight, so he couldn't come himself, but he wanted me to tell you that he loves you like mad. Like Beauty and the Beast. Like Cinderella and the prince. Like—"

"I get the picture." Ariel touched two fingers to the sudden pounding in her temples. She was getting the picture, all right, but she didn't like it. Apparently the lecture she'd given Patrice about being "only friends" with Josh had disappeared in the fuzzy matter between her ears.

"Aw, hell," Killer muttered in a perfect imitation of her dad. "I didn't know you had company. Am I gonna be in your way? Because I'm not supposed to stay if I'm being a pest."

Jeanne had shown up in the doorway. It usually took a bomb to get her offtrack from murder and mayhem, but the child clearly captured her interest. She glanced at Ariel, then the flowers, then the child. "You're not interrupting anything, sweetie. I'm just family. And a friend of Ariel's. And you're—?"

"Patrice Anne Penoyer. But everybody calls me Killer. Nice to meet you," she said politely, and then spotted the brownies.

Ariel sighed, then dug in the cupboard for another plate.

"I like those flowers," Jeanne said admiringly.

"Yeah, aren't they great? They're from my dad. For Ariel. Because he loves her, you know, like Cinderella and the prince, and—"

"And here I didn't even know that Ariel had someone new in her life." Jeanne glanced meaningfully at Ariel again. "You like stories, do you? That's what I do for a living, make up stories. I'm a writer."

"Oh, yeah? You mean you write stuff like fairy tales?"

"Well, actually, the stuff I write tends to be about serial killers."

"I can get into that," Killer assured her. "Just this morning, I was ready to kill my cereal. Spilled the milk when I was pouring it. By the time I got it all cleaned up, the pops were all squishy and soggy and yucky, and Cal, he just said, 'tough luck, squirt.'"

When both women chuckled, Killer looked startled, and then abruptly pleased. By the time she'd devoured a brownie buried in ice cream and three maraschino cherries, Jeanne had her complete life story and Ariel sneaked back in the kitchen for some aspirin. The vague tightening in her temples had turned into a three-hammer doozy of a headache.

This wasn't happening, she told herself. She'd told the urchin that she wasn't marrying her dad. She'd explained how dads can sometimes have women friends who were just pals. And none of the kids, even once, had seen Josh lay a finger on her. There was just no basis, no *reason*, why Killer should still be harboring expectations about her and her father.

She downed two aspirin, dry. When she hustled back into the living room, though, she wished she hadn't. Killer and Jeanne were stretched out on pillows on the floor, looking like a matched set of derelict orphans and talking thick as thieves.

"We're close." Killer was apparently explaining her relationship to Ariel by crossing two fingers together. "*That* close. Which is why I came by. To give her the flowers from my dad, but also 'cause I had to talk to her."

Ariel stepped in then. "What about, honey? What's wrong?"

"School is what's wrong. Dad says it's time to get enrolled for first grade. And I gotta have shots at the doctor's before I can do that. He took me to the school yesterday morning to look around. I looked around. I'm not going, and no way I'm having those shots. Nobody, but nobody is gonna talk me into having any shots, so I figured you could talk to him." Killer turned back to Jeanne, confiding, "Ariel could prob'ly make my dad do anything, because they're real close, you know?" Her crossed fingers shot up in the air again to illustrate. "*That* close. He'd about do anything for her...."

Ariel sank in the overstuffed chair and briefly considered clicking her heels three times. Disappearing to Kansas struck her as a great idea, and the click-heels trick had certainly worked for Dorothy.

"Ariel?" Killer piped up.

"What, love bug?"

"I gotta go potty."

Once the child had been shown the bathroom, her friend just looked at her. "You've been holding out on me."

"No, I haven't. Damnation." The two aspirin were stuck in her throat like burrs. No way she could swallow. "She's a darling, and I love her, but somehow she's got this idea that she wants me for a mother. Actually, I thought the problem was all fixed. Apparently not."

"Nothing going on between you and the dad?"

"Heavens, no. He's been as embarrassed by this little dilemma as I have."

"How...interesting." Jeanne ruthlessly studied her face. "You sure there's nothing going on? That little monkey sure seems positive that her dad and you—"

"For Pete's sake," Ariel said crossly. "He's recently divorced, has three kids and is scrambling real hard to keep his family together. He's not looking for anyone, and you know how I feel about marriage. You *know* me."

"Yeah, I do. You have a habit of picking up strays and adopting them as family. Like me. Like everyone around you. You can't stand it when anyone is alone or left out, but sometime, one of these years, I figured some guy was gonna notice that you happen to be a peach who could use a little adopting herself."

"I'm not a piece of fruit and I don't need adopting. You have this all wrong—" The ringing of the telephone cut off the discussion. She reached back for the receiver on the far lamp table, and slapped it against her ear. "Hello?"

There was a man's voice on the other end. A husky tenor that she didn't need identified, and tonight he sounded gut tired. "Is she there?"

Ariel closed her eyes. Josh didn't have to identify who he was talking about, either. "Yes."

"Aw, hell. The baby-sitter left at seven, and she slipped the noose on the boys. If she's driving you crazy—"

"She's not, Josh. She's no trouble at all. And I'll make sure she gets home before dark. But..."

"But?"

Eyes still closed, she scrunched up her nose as if she were holding her breath before diving into murky deep waters. "But I'm just not exactly, precisely, positively sure we've...um...solved our problem. About me. About her thinking that you and me—"

"I'm getting the same nonsense triple-time from the boys. Daily doses of singing your praises, and the thirteen-year-old's suddenly coaching me about dating." Josh sighed, heavily and loud. "Well, I could kill all three of them if you want. Especially my youngest. You want me to drown my baby?''

''Well . . . I'm pretty fond of her.''

''Yeah, me, too,'' he said disgustedly, ''but maybe there's an alternative. I could send her off to a convent. I've been thinking about doing that anyway, until she's forty or so. I can't even con her into going to school, so there's no way I'm going to survive her teenage years. You think a convent's a good idea?''

''I think you'd miss her to death.''

''That's true, but it leaves us back at square one. Killer's got you on a pedestal so high that I just don't know how to get you knocked off the hot seat. I wouldn't blame you for being real exasperated. Listen . . .''

She was listening. Her blue living room had taken on smoky sunset shadows; Patrice had skipped back in and was volubly explaining to Jeanne about Boober, her imaginary friend. Ariel was right there, rationally aware of everything around her, but oddly the only connection she felt was through Ma Bell and the husky, winsome dry humor in Josh's voice.

''I suspect you've had enough of us, especially my youngest, but I keep thinking about what you said. About if the kids just kept seeing us together, behaving like nothing more than casual friends, they'd eventually have to get the message.''

''I still think that's true,'' she said hesitantly.

''So maybe we could try it one more time? Something easy, something simple. Just some outing where we could all get together and they could see you as . . . well, as a friend. Like maybe we could go . . . bowling.''

''Bowling?''

"Dumb idea, huh? I should have known you wouldn't do anything like that—"

Her eyebrows arched. There was just something in Penoyer's voice that pegged her as a spoiled Persian kitten, too hotsy-totsy to do anything as mundane as bowling. "That sounds fine," she said firmly.

"You sure? I just thought of it on the spur of the moment. We could do something else. For that matter, I don't want you to feel on the spot to do anything at all—"

"I love bowling. I've always loved bowling. The whole idea sounds great to me," she assured him. That wasn't precisely true, but how hard could it be to stick your fingers in a couple of holes and roll a ball down an alley? And it wasn't as if she were volunteering for more trouble. This proposed outing had absolutely nothing to do with her confused and unsettling feelings for Josh—it was about his kids.

Ariel understood, better than anyone, how children were knocked for six after a divorce. And although technically his kids weren't her business or her problem, from the start she'd felt both involved and responsible. It wasn't another woman that Patrice had chosen to attach herself to. It was her. How could she not try and resolve a problem that somehow she had helped create?

After making arrangements with Josh for Saturday afternoon, she hung up the phone. Oddly enough, her headache had completely disappeared . . . at least until she suddenly noticed her old friend staring at her with a big, fat grin.

"So," Jeanne said gravely, "there's nothing going on between the two of you, huh?" And then bent over double on a hoot of laughter.

"You don't understand," Ariel said testily. There was no point in explaining, not while her friend—her ex-friend—was still cackling like a sick witch.

She rubbed a hand over her face, a gesture that she vaguely realized was something Josh did all the time. Her unconsciously picking up his gesture struck her as oddly reassuring. Never mind everyone else. Never mind what the whole damn world thought, for that matter. *She* understood exactly why they were getting together. And so, she thought, did Josh.

Damned if Josh knew how he'd come up with this bowling outing idea. He couldn't think straight around the woman. Even talking to her on the phone, the strangest confounded things seemed to come out of his mouth, nothing he ever intended or planned. Being around her in person, the problem was even worse.

Much worse.

Josh climbed out of the Bronco. The kids had already belted out the doors and were galloping toward the entrance of the bowling alley. It wasn't the first Saturday afternoon his crew had spent rolling a few balls, but Josh would bet the bank it wasn't a familiar experience for Ms. Lindstrom.

She was staring at the building with an enthusiastic smile—the fakest enthusiastic smile he'd ever seen. "You haven't been here before?" he asked.

"Not this specific bowling alley," she admitted.

He believed that. Her choice of clothes, in fact, struck him as just a teensy off kilter for anyone who'd ever played the sport. There was nothing wrong with her sandals—they showed off her slim ankles and calves and long, bare legs. Only, he wasn't sure how they were going to rent shoes for her, when she wasn't wearing socks.

The rest of her outfit consisted of a little skirty pair of shorts and a loose, scooped-neck top. Both were in a wild splashy print, but the style was certainly modest in design—as long as she was standing up straight. No one had to be a pro athlete to bowl, but for sure you had to bend over to throw the ball.

If she bent over, that scooped neck was going to generously dip—unless Josh filched some tape from the guy behind the counter and pasted the material to her chest. Somehow he didn't think she'd take to that idea. Somehow he didn't think she intentionally planned to flash the gang with the color of her underpants every time she threw the ball. And somehow he was becoming increasingly damn sure that she'd never been bowling before.

"You know, I never meant for you to feel conned into this. You can still back out. If it isn't something you feel comfortable doing, we could—"

"Josh, there's no reason for you to keep apologizing. I couldn't think of a more perfect idea in a million years. It's public. Something that all ages do together. Nothing romantic about it. And we really *have* to do something to cut off those wild ideas in Killer's head about the two of us. This is an ideal environment for her to see me as a pal, a crony, a friend—you know, just one of the guys."

Just one of the guys? At his own requiem mass, Josh doubted he'd be able to see her as "one of the guys." He cleared his throat as he pushed open the glass door. "Speaking of Killer . . . I think my daughter has something confused. She says you have a friend who's a serial killer."

Ariel chuckled. "Patrice just met a writer friend of mine. Actually, Jeanne is more family than friend. She's my mom's second husband's sister's ex-husband's third cousin—"

"Stop." He raised a hand for mercy. He'd heard her explain the convoluted relationships of her family before. "I'll hustle over and rent a lane. What size shoes do you wear?"

"Shoes?" She looked at him blankly.

He said patiently, "They keep the shoes behind the counter. We need to rent you a pair. You can't wear street shoes or sandals past that line." He motioned.

"Of course. I knew that," she said swiftly. Then she added with a grin, "Size eight...I have big feet. Heaven's it's really noisy in here."

"Uh-huh." Bowling alleys weren't exactly known for funereal silence. Balls were rhythmically cracking down pins. Kids were racing all over the place. It looked as if a league of senior citizen gals had taken over the right side, but even with the place unusually crowded, there were still a couple of free lanes right in front of the door.

He glanced at Ariel, who hadn't budged from his side and was studying the scene as if it were an unfamiliar snake pit. "Honey?" The endearment just slipped out. "You see where the kids are?"

"Yes." Abruptly she spotted the three familiar heads. "I'll go take care of them while you're renting the shoes and lanes and things," she assured him.

Josh suspected his urchins would take care of her, instead of the other way around. Still, while he paid at the front counter, he kept his head half turned to watch out for her. His kids knew the routine, and had already claimed a lane by dropping their gear. Patrice was picking out a ball in the squirt-size section. Just occasionally, he got a few signs he was raising the boys right, because Cal and Bruiser were courteously coaching Ariel as they helped her pick out a ball.

It took a few minutes to get the crew settled in, shoes on, score sheet set up, balls chosen. The guy behind the counter had Peds, taking care of Ariel's sockless problem, and she was chattering with Killer ten for a dozen as they tied their shoes. Not that he didn't trust her judgment, but he lifted her ball to check it out. It struck him as a superb choice. For a three-hundred-pound man. "You don't think this is a little heavy for you?" he asked her.

"I always like a heavy ball," she assured him.

Uh-huh. "Would you like to go first?"

"No," she said swiftly. "You guys get started, and I'll just bring up the rear with Patrice."

"I always go first, Ariel, because I'm the girl," Patrice promptly informed her.

"Well, I'll just watch the rest of you and bring up the rear anyway," Ariel said.

Josh watched her studying the proceedings with the intensity of a judge in a courtroom. Killer decided she'd wait and "go next to Ariel," so Bruiser stepped up first, starting off with a spare that earned him a clap on the back from the clan. Cal rolled a gutter ball, but made it up on the second try by socking down eight. Josh took his turn, but then stayed on his feet to coach the squirt. He had his doubts she'd ever hit a pin in this lifetime, but she was a born ham, first dramatically squinching up her face, then squinting at the faraway pins, then taking her pint-size steps with an appalling swish of her six-year-old hips before letting loose. The ball, predictably, bounced down the lane, veered, curved, re-veered and then plopped in the gutter.

"Good try, baby, good try." Josh thumped her on the back.

"Good try," Ariel echoed. "You did great, sweetie!"

The boys gave Patrice encouragement, too—Josh'd have killed them if they hadn't—but eventually that minor ruckus died down. They waited patiently, until Ariel seemed to abruptly realize they were staring at her and leapt to her feet.

"It's my turn, huh? I mean ... of course it is!" she said with a laugh.

That moment, that exact moment, Josh realized he was in love with her. The sudden fist clenching his heart, the sick scary feeling in his gut ... denial wasn't getting him anywhere. His eyes wouldn't let her alone. His mind stayed tuned to her channel. Somehow she'd stolen a fat chunk of his soul and nothing, but nothing, was the same when she wasn't around. He wasn't sure how it happened. He was even less sure what to do about it—or if he was going to be insane enough to do anything—but damned if he could deny that huge, raw, terrifying well of emotion for her.

He watched her step up to the ball. First she doused a little talcum on her fingers, exactly, he mused, the way she'd watched him do. She fitted her fingers in the monster-size ball, her frown already pinched in concentration as she turned to face the pins. She looked just like a pro, like she'd done this a hundred times, but every single movement she made was a mimic of something she'd seen him or the boys do.

Her hair tucked in the curve of her neck when she bent over, concentrating hard, giving him a hopelessly alluring view of her rump in those bitsy skirt-shorts. She lifted the ball. Compressed her mouth. Took three steps. Swung the ball back.

"Holy kamoly!" Bruiser yelped.

"Oh my God, oh my God," Cal groaned.

Josh was already up and moving. Guilt added adrenaline to his speed—*dammit,* he'd known the finger holes in that ball were too big for her—but unfortunately, the horse was already out of the barn. She had a lot of force and momentum going when she swung the bowling ball back. So when it slipped free, it kept flying.

Not in the direction of the pins, but toward *them!*

Cal leapt out of the way, and Josh gave his son credit for fast reflexes. Only, that left nothing in the missile's path. It was hardly traveling at jet speed, but the basic physics principle applied about a heavy object in motion. It wanted to stay in motion.

The ball slapped into the glass entrance door, which finally stopped the sucker. For a millisecond, Josh thought—he prayed—everything was going to be okay. Everyone in the alley had stopped playing and was staring at those doors just as he was. The glass seemed secure for a second.

Then it cracked.

One long lightning crack down the center followed, regretfully, by a noisy tinkling splinter as the whole bottom of the door shattered.

Eight

Josh had made dinner. Mac and cheese. Chops. Peas. Nobody was eating the peas, which was hardly headliner news, but no one was eating anything else, either. He hadn't protested when the squirt set a plate for her confounded imaginary friend, hadn't climbed on anybody about manners, but it hadn't helped. Nothing was helping. Cal and Bruiser were hunched over their plates and Killer kept squishing peas with her spoon, staring at him with woebegone eyes.

"Come on, everybody. Eat," Josh said firmly. "Ariel's got a good sense of humor and—thank you, God—she never had any life ambitions to be a bowler. There's no reason to act like some major tragedy occurred. We got her to laugh about it, didn't we?"

"I just don't think you shoulda left her, Dad," Bruiser said.

"She wanted to go home."

"Yeah, but I think she only wanted to go home because she was embarrassed half to death." Calvin stabbed a macaroni noodle with his fork, but he didn't eat it.

"I thought it was neat," Patrice piped up. "It was like magic, you know. One minute, sunshine was shining in the glass door. The next minute, crash, boom, tinkle, and everybody was shouting and running—"

"Shut up, squirt."

"Shut up, squirt."

"Don't say 'shut up' to your sister." Scolding the boys about their language was automatic. Sometimes they even listened, but at the moment, Josh suspected, they wouldn't have heard a brass band playing right outside the window. Nothing was going to divert their minds from Ariel.

"I really don't get it." Bruiser waved his knife. "She didn't know how to bowl, did she? She didn't know how to play at all. So why didn't she just tell us that to begin with?"

"Yeah," Calvin agreed. "How come she made out like she'd bowled a million times?"

"You're asking me? As if I'm supposed to know? For four thousand years," Josh informed his sons, "men have been trying to figure out why women do things. Don't hold your breath assuming there's ever a simple answer."

"Well, I think it's simple," Patrice said. "Ariel thought bowling was something we liked, so she fibbed. She was trying to be nice because she loves us."

"Shut up, squirt."

"Shut up, squirt." Calvin echoed the insult to his sister by rote, but clearly his heart wasn't in it. He looked straight at his dad. "The owner . . . he sure was mad."

"I know." Josh swiped a hand over his face. Dinner hours were never restful, but this one was turning into an all-star ulcer. He'd already mentally replayed the afternoon's debacle. He wasn't happy, not about anything that happened, but the kids rehashing the event was only making him feel worse.

"For a while there, I thought you were gonna hit the guy." Bruiser's face mirrored disappointment that this exciting possibility hadn't come to pass.

"I was never going to hit him. I've told you, boys. Violence is never an effective way to settle a problem. And he didn't mean any of that language toward Ariel personally. He was upset. So he let loose. He had every right to be upset, every right to let a little loose—"

"But Ariel was getting all shook up when he started yelling at her," Calvin said.

"I *know* she was shook up. That's why I chose to have a few private words with him." Josh saw no reason to discuss the exact nature of that conversation. The whole thing had taken place behind the slammed door of the owner's office. If the exchange had become a wee bit heated, Ariel hadn't been exposed to it. And neither had his kids. "Anyway, it's over. The door'll be paid for. As long as Ariel—please, God— doesn't plan on joining any bowling leagues in the near future, there's no problem. Nothing left to talk about. It's time to forget it."

"I don't think Ariel's forgot it," Patrice said.

"I think you should do something, Dad," Calvin said.

"Me, too," Bruiser agreed.

Josh gave up attempting to eat and glared at his offspring. "What? You're driving me all crazy, for cripes' sake. What exactly is it that you think I should do?"

"We think..." Calvin's careful tone reflected how often he'd orchestrated the spokesman role for his siblings before. "...we think that you should do something to make her feel better. Like go over and see her."

The Bronco was one sturdily built truck. It took a lot to rattle the chassis. When Josh climbed out and slammed the door, the chassis rattled good.

Damn kids.

Hands on hips, he scowled up at Ariel's apartment windows. Curtains were drawn and the place was dark, but a sliver of light peeked through a crack and her red MG was parked in the alleyway. The odds leaned toward her being home, but he wouldn't bet with a bookie on the odds of her wanting to see him. And he still wasn't sure how his blasted kids had talked him into coming here.

He tucked in his shirt and finger-brushed his hair, knowing he was stalling because any grooming or fix-ups were an exercise in futility.

Storm clouds were whipping across the sky, burying the half-moon, and the night wind was strong enough to toss his hair and leaves and anything else that wasn't tied down. He trudged across the parking lot to her back metal stairs, wishing he could be handily tied down. Somewhere else. Like Alaska or the North Pole. Anywhere but here.

At home, they were out of milk, and five loads of wash were mounded on the laundry room floor. Josh only had the weekend to get all the nuisance chores done. Besides that, he'd always given himself credit for being good—even great—at certain things. Like electrical schematics, and getting a work crew to hustle, and loving his kids. But how he was supposed to make a lady feel better for throwing a bowling ball through a glass door...

No. He positively had no experience or skills in this type of thing. Somehow the kids had made him feel guilty. Somehow the manipulative devils he'd spawned had gotten the outlandish idea that dads were, by definition, heroes. Dads fixed things that went wrong. It was their job. Dads were never scared of nightmares; they never ran away from tough problems, and they might yell, but you could always count on dads to take care of people.

Josh always believed that part of his parenting job was teaching his kids ethical behavior... but that was yesterday. Before those damn-fool values had been turned against him.

Abruptly he loosened the choking-tight collar of his shirt. At least the kids didn't know—couldn't know—that he was in love with her. They had a right to expect a certain paternal behavior out of him, but so far, positively, he hadn't had a single paternal thought regarding Ariel.

He trudged up the metal stairs, still undecided about whether he was going to knock when he reached the top. He could still take a powder. He could still disappear before she realized he was there.

Likely he was gonna make a fool of himself, bumble out something inadequate or turn tongue-tied—but that kind of humiliation wouldn't kill him. Discovering he was in love with her, though, made him feel wary, uneasy, shaken. Nothing had changed in his life. He still had a job, three kids, responsibilities and commitments that allowed no time for romancing a woman. Especially a woman who already personally, directly, knew that his kids and his life were a passel of trouble.

He couldn't think of a single reason why Ariel would willingly want to take them all on. Which meant he'd sure as hell better keep a tight lid on his emotions, his actions—and for damn sure, his hormones.

Ariel didn't hear a knock. When the blow dryer was screeching on high, she probably wouldn't hear a tornado. Twice a week, she swore she was going to whack off her hair. She'd never grown it long out of vanity, but because it was just too fine to hold a style, so wearing it simple, straight and long had solved a problem. Still, the ritual of washing and drying long hair was a royal time-consuming pain.

She had no reason to suddenly shut off the hair dryer. The ends were dry and flying in the dryer's gale wind, but the crown was still damp. It would take another full five minutes of arm-aching brushing and fussing before the job was done. Yet she flicked the off switch with a sudden perplexed frown.

When the whine of the dryer died, the apartment was still. The bathroom was still fragrant and foggy with mist from her recent shower. She could hear the clock ticking in the kitchen, and outside, the fretful whistle of wind from the coming storm. It was going to be a thunder-clapping deluge, Ariel expected, which was fine with her. She loved storms—the wilder the better. Maybe the storm explained this sudden, restless feeling of anticipation.

She set down the dryer and hooked her arms into a short, silky kimono. The fabric felt shivery-cool on her bare skin, raising goose bumps. After tying the sash, she pulled her hair free from the neck and ambled barefoot, first through the hall and living room, then toward the kitchen.

She only pushed aside the curtain to glance outside and check the progress of the storm. A scissor of lightning clipped the sky, riveting her attention—until she caught the shadowed figure outside her back door and almost jumped out of her skin. For a second. The thick black hair, the shoulders, the sharp blade of a profile were so familiar that she didn't need lightning—or light—to identify Josh.

He saw her face through the curtain. In the freeze-frame of a moment, their eyes met, and suddenly her heart was hammering, loud and hard.

She dropped the curtain, zipped to the door and yanked the bolt. She'd just pulled open the door when the sky let loose the first thick, fat spatters of rain. "I never heard you knock! You nearly scared me half to death. For heaven's sake, get in before the storm hits—"

He stepped in, but no farther than it took to close the door in the minivestibule. The kitchen had turned gloomy dark; she hadn't taken time to switch on a light, but his gaze lasered on her short robe and her bare legs and damp hair. Moments before, she'd felt shivering cool. One look from his eyes was as effective as the hot blast from a furnace, but he wasn't budging from the doorway. "I can see you were in the shower. I should have called before coming—"

"It's okay. I was just thinking about making a pot of tea. I'll put on the kettle, and then if you don't mind being deserted for a minute, I'll pull some clothes on." She yanked the light chain over the sink and reached for the teakettle. The yellow light fell on his face. Her heart skipped, then thudded a hammer beat again.

"It really is all right," she said quietly. "I know why you're here."

His eyebrows wedged in an arch. "Well, you're one up on me then, because damned if I can explain what I was doing on your doorstep."

It was so like him, the gruffness, the dry humor directed at himself, even the direct sexual awareness of his gaze. Ariel felt a huge, engulfing wave of pure emotion. It would go away. She'd been telling herself all afternoon and evening that it would go away. It always did. If there was anything she understood in life, it was love. No different than catching an unpredictable flu, no matter how sure you were going to die from it, the symptoms were temporary and untrustworthy and always, eventually passed.

After that crazy clown scene in the bowling alley, Ariel couldn't believe the clamp wasn't already secure on those feelings.

She turned the burner under the teakettle to high. "I thought you knew you could be honest with me," she said swiftly.

"Honest with you?"

"Come on, Josh. I'm not surprised you're here. I'd have made the same visit if I were in your shoes." She reached in the cupboard for two cups, then glanced at him. "I didn't ask if you actually wanted tea. I don't think I have beer, but I probably have some wine around. Or lemonade—"

"Are you deliberately trying to confuse me?"

"About the choices of what there is around to drink—?"

He squeezed his eyes closed and swiped a hand over his face. "Ariel. I don't care if I drink mud. Could we just start this conversation over? You seem real sure you know why I'm here—"

"You're angry with me."

"You think I'm *mad* at you?"

"Maybe not *mad* exactly. But ticked. Irked. Disappointed. And with reason, Josh. Believe me, I understand." She ducked her head. Plopping two tea bags in the cups took all her concentration. Far too much concentration to look at him. "I really thought it was a good idea for them to see us together. I really thought...well, that the kids seemed to be missing an adult woman in their lives, someone who wasn't their mom but who could maybe be a different kind of role model. Pretty ridiculous. I'm no mom, and I haven't got a role model in my whole background that could give me a clue about what your kids need. The proof of that was really in the pudding, wasn't it? I really muffed it with the kids this afternoon. They probably don't ever want to see me again. I don't blame them. Heck, I lied to them, embarrassed them, probably embarrassed you, too—"

"Ariel?"

"What?" The teakettle screamed. She whisked it off the stove and turned off the burner.

"You reached all those conclusions from a short half hour of bowling?"

"Come on, Josh. You feel uneasy about me being around your kids. Isn't that what you came to tell me?"

"Actually…" She wasn't sure when he loosened the death grip he'd had on her back doorknob and started coming toward her. "Actually, I *did* come because of the kids. They sent me to do their scud work. That's the truth. They seemed to think I'd have the guts—and the tact—to break it to you gently. We all feel pretty strongly, sweet pea, that you don't have a lot of future in the sport of bowling. We just think you'd be better off taking up a hobby that didn't involve big, heavy balls. 'Course, if I'm hurting your feelings with this news, the kids're gonna slay me alive—"

"Josh."

"Hmm?"

She dunked the tea bags in the boiling water, but her eyes were on his face. "They're not mad at me?"

"Nope. Although I'd advise you to shore up some fortitude, because they're probably going to tease you for months. Something like this happens, Penoyers don't have a real good record of showing mercy. It's too damned much fun to keep dredging the victim over the coals. I'd say the chances of them forgetting it are—ballpark—a billion to one."

"Josh?"

"Hmm?"

Although her gaze never shifted from his face, she was still dunking, dunking, dunking those tea bags. "Okay, so the kids might have thought it was funny, but I doubt you did. You have to feel … disappointed in me? For letting you down?"

His eyes didn't *really* darken, because obviously a person's eyes had no possible way to change color. But in that bead of a moment—maybe it was a trick of light—his familiar melted chocolate-brown eyes seemed to take on the fire of ebony. "Clearly, I'm failing to communicate here. No surprise. I was never real hot with words. You think you could manage to put down those tea bags for two seconds?"

"What tea bags?"

"My point exactly. Your mind isn't on tea. And I swore to myself I wouldn't do this. I swore. And I meant it. But dammit, Ariel, this is your fault. I don't know where you got that harebrained idea about letting me down, but it's stupid, you hear me?"

She heard him. Apparently, though, Josh hadn't heard anything about the New Age sensitive man, because a politically correct lover these days would never call a woman "stupid"—and certainly not before he tried to kiss her. Of course, more than conceivably, Josh had never planned to kiss her. Heaven knew, she wasn't any more prepared than he was.

He swooped so quickly that she barely had a chance to drop the tea bags. His mouth took hers, claimed hers, with a dizzying pressure that made her neck arch back. Tipsy butterflies bounced off the walls in her stomach. Every feminine nerve seemed to suffer a sudden electric charge. Josh may not be hot with words, but he had no trouble communicating nonverbally that he was mad—frustrated and exasperated. With her.

She understood completely. All afternoon and evening, she'd felt that exact kind of anger—with herself.

She'd let him down. Something that never should have happened. Her whole life, she'd carefully avoided the type of sticky, tangling relationships in which hurting someone else was inevitable. Her parents had begun every marriage with a hat full of expectations, always believing the new love would last, always blind-sure that the right mate was the answer to all their needs. No one could do that, which Ariel had under-stood for forever. Get anywhere near someone's ex-pectations, and you were bound to hurt them.

She hadn't realized, until their little bowling fiasco that afternoon, how much she'd come to feel for Josh. Her ludicrous aim with the blasted ball wasn't the problem—as long as no one was hurt, that part had almost been humorous. But she hadn't come home laughing. She'd come home feeling heartsick and un-settled...and scared. How had it happened, that she'd allowed herself to care so much that letting Josh down felt like a crushing mountain? He'd trusted her with his kids. He'd counted on her to be a guide, a helpful adult female influence for his kids. And she'd blown it.

Thunder cracked open the sky with a loud boom, so close it made the house shake. The light bulb over the sink winked off.

Josh framed her face in his hands, stealing another kiss from her as if he never noticed the sudden dark-ness. A second flash of lightning silvered the whole side of his face. He didn't seem aware of that, either.

"You still think you let me down? You still think you screwed up with me? Dammit, Ariel. Do I have to carve it in stone for you to figure out how I feel about you?"

Maybe he was still swearing. But his voice had turned whiskey-low, the anger gone, something raw-soft and husky in its place. Rain rattled down the windows in a noisy, gusty torrent, confusing her, distracting her.

He was supposed to be mad. She understood mad. She didn't understand what was happening now at all.

Her spine was still wedged in the vee of the kitchen counter. The electricity in the air still created a powerhouse of tension, but in the whisper of a moment, his mouth had softened on hers.

This was fire, but a deeper, darker fire. Rough, urgent kisses had suddenly turned burning slow. These kisses were givers, not takers. He rubbed, savoring her unique taste, her unique texture, communicating a reverence and tenderness that she had no idea Josh felt for her. One kiss seeped into another, knit and tangled into another and another, each one more coaxing-slow than the last. Each one more arousing.

She didn't know when she started kissing him back. She didn't know if he realized how much aching loneliness he was revealing to her. Her fingertips touched his whiskered jaw, and then swept around his neck, pulling him down, pulling him to her. Her breasts crushed against him, cradled tight against his heartbeat. Blood galloped through her veins when she felt the hardness and heat of his arousal. She recognized danger. All day, she'd understood that her emotions for Josh had already dipped in the danger zone, and she was smart. So smart that she'd always brilliantly avoided trouble she couldn't handle.

But he was wounded, her Josh. And lonely. She knew about those life wounds; she understood that kind of aching loneliness. Denied feelings bubbled up like air trapped in water; repressed needs careened past her guard. He was the only man who'd ever aroused either. She wanted to be his answer. She wanted to be his anchor. And damn Josh, because he was making her believe that she could be.

His mouth tore free from hers. He leaned his forehead against her forehead, both of them breathing harder than if they'd outrun a pack of thieves. "Say no, Ariel."

His whisper touched her more intimately than the palm sweeping her back. He didn't want her to say no. "I have some protection in my nightstand. It's probably buried pretty far back in the drawer. I haven't had any need to look for it in a while."

"That isn't the question I was asking you, sweet pea."

She knew the question he was asking. She also suspected she was short on time to consider her choices. The way he looked at her was fire. The way he touched her was lighting a series of explosive fuses.

She reached her hands between them to unbutton his shirt. Two buttons loosened, but the third caught on a thread. Her fingers fumbled, not because it was too dark to see the shirt, but because her eyes never left his face.

"Ariel..." He said her name like a dire warning, but damned if it didn't sound like a calling, too.

She couldn't seem to loosen that third button, so she just pulled it. The button popped and sailed across the room. So did his shirt, seconds later.

He pushed off one shoe in the kitchen; the other was abandoned in the hall doorway along with his belt. Her sash made it to the knob on the bathroom door, but her robe slithered in a heap just inside her bedroom. She was naked for those few seconds while he shucked off his jeans. Alone and naked. Shivery, vulnerably naked.

But not for long. Spears of lightning flashed, illuminating the tense—intense—lines of his face. It didn't take him a countdown second to get rid of those jeans, and even less time to yank off the comforter and toss the pillows on the carpet. Then he came for her.

Her emerald-green sheets looked black in the dim light, almost as black as his eyes as he lowered her down. The sheet fabric was satin-cold against her skin, but Josh's whole body was hotter than a furnace. If she was shivering, it wasn't from the texture or temperature of those sheets.

The rain beat down the windows in staccato pellets. She barely heard the storm over the wild, keening drum in her ears.

Her bedroom was a feminine haven—lush deep colors, almond and rose petals in a potpourri bowl by the bed, a silk chemise draped on a chair, earrings and jewelry strewn on the chest. She noticed those things only because the man coming apart in her arms was such a contrast.

Bristly hair, wiry, completely unlike her own unmanageably fine hair, covered his chest. His arms and shoulders were sleek and hard, muscled where she had none, tense where every bone in her body seemed liquid. He wasn't unshaven, but this late at night, his chin was rough and tickly with stubble. His hands were bigger than hers, bigger and callused and never, even for a second, still.

"In the nightstand—" she whispered.

She'd never aroused that lazy, dangerous smile before. "We'll get to that," he said. "Later."

She couldn't imagine what he meant by later. Later was an hour ago. Later was a dozen years ago, when she still had claim on a few wits. She'd guessed he'd be a wild lover. She'd guessed—her nerves had worried—that he'd be different than any other man she'd known. Making love with Josh could well be a frightening and uncomfortable experience, best thought out very carefully—a lady didn't unleash a tiger unless she was prepared for the repercussions.

All those instinctive feminine worries—every one of them—proved true. She regularly found fairy dust in a Connecticut summer night, inhaled the magic of carnivals and fortune-telling, loved creating illusions with scarves and smoking mirrors. But the primitive, pagan emotions Josh aroused in her was enchantment of an entirely different color magic.

His hands, mouth, tongue swept her body—the sensitive inside of her thigh, the flat plane of her abdomen, the crease in her knee. No body part escaped his touch. His caresses were earthy, urgent, exploring spy missions that deliberately sought what aroused her, then used those discoveries to make her ache, make her want, make her miserable with frustrated desire.

She didn't like it. Feeling this fragile and come-apart vulnerable, feeling this shaky and feverish, feeling as if she'd lost her whole sense of gravity. She found his mouth, kissed him hard, her blood rushing with impatience and never-expected fear, some stupid feminine fear she couldn't even name. That she'd be taken under? That she'd never be the same?

He smiled at her, right after that kiss. Smiled, and then dived right back for another.

The sheets rumpled and twisted beneath them. He pulled her on top of him, where her full weight was pressed intimately against him, where he had access to her spine and fanny for more of those wild, long, slow caresses. And then he rolled and pulled her beneath him, teasing her with his weight. His body slickened, so did hers. He caught her wrists, pinned them above her head, lavished kisses on her throat and breasts until she curled up, legs swinging, to trap and capture him closer.

She'd known he was a physical, emotional man, just never anticipated how much trouble that meant. He seemed to take it for granted, the lusty enjoyment of her body, of sex, of every scent and sound and touch, as if nothing else existed in this moment but her. He would know her, like no other lover knew her. No one was escaping this bed with an inhibition that hadn't been trampled to dust.

In some vague blur, she saw him reach in her nightstand and finger-search blind in the drawer. He found the packet way in the back, left the drawer gaping open. Even that instant's separation infuriated both of them. With his eyes on her face, he took care of the condom, then took care of her, wrapping her legs around him tight before plunging, hard and deep, inside her. In those luminous dark eyes, she saw a man ready to explode, a man overloading on need and desire, a man who'd pushed himself way, way over the civilized edge.

She took him in. She took him down. There was no soothing him, not in those silky dark waters, but that drowning dive had the rush of a waterfall, the surge and power of total immersion. Total immersion . . . in him.

"I love you, Josh." The words were impossible to hold back. There was no way she could hold anything back—not words, not emotions, not anything of herself. "Love you," she repeated on the hush of a cry, then hissed his name as flames shot through those deep waters. Her whole body convulsed, riding the shuddering wave of those flames.

Nine

The storm was over. Moonlight spilled through the window, creating misty squares of white on the bed and carpet. The whole night had turned dusty quiet and still. Josh turned his head to read the dial on the nightstand clock.

The battery clock claimed it was a few minutes after eleven.

The thing had to be lying. The time *had* to be later than eleven. How could his whole life seem inalterably changed in just a few short hours?

Anxiety chugalugged through his pulse. His heartbeat refused to settle down. He'd known that making love to Ariel would be dangerous. He'd *known*. Did a grown man play with electric cords? Did a mature, intelligent man go for a stroll in a forest fire?

Ariel stirred, murmuring a sleepy sigh. She'd uncovered her shoulders. Again. Protectively he tucked the sheet around her—again—and snuggled her closer. Absently he started stroking her hair, threading his fingers through the silky strands in a rhythmic, soothing caress, thinking man, she was trouble.

He felt as if someone had kicked him upside the head, and he just couldn't seem to recover from the blow.

He'd never planned on making love with her… although he could pinpoint the exact moment when his common sense had turned to dust. They'd been in the kitchen when the damn woman had started talking about letting him down. It was as if a mousetrap had sprung in his brain. He just couldn't stand it, her thinking that she'd disappointed him, her believing that she'd failed him. So he'd kissed her. And there was absolutely nothing ethically or morally wrong with kissing her. It was just that three hours had passed since that first, single, exasperated kiss, and he was still reeling from the consequences.

Ariel had more passion and sensuality concentrated in a compact one-hundred-and-twenty-pound package than any woman he'd ever met—but that wasn't the problem. An experienced man knew how to yank the reins on chemistry and hormones. It was magic that he'd never expected, magic he'd never believed in—and nohow, no way, was he prepared for.

She was a dream lover. *His* dream lover. Josh expected that every man indulged in fantasies from time to time. On long, dark, lonely nights it was just something a guy did—imagined a beautiful woman coming on to him, a free-spirited, wildly exciting lover with no inhibitions, a woman who burned up the night because she was that hot, uniquely and only, for him. Every man had fantasies like that in the back of his mind. They were nothing Josh had ever worried about. It was just a guy thing.

Only, tarnation, a man's fantasies were never supposed to come true.

"Josh?"

He swallowed fast. It seemed the woman who'd made him forget rhyme, reason, life, gravity—and all claim to sanity—was coming awake. "Hmm?"

"I feel *wonderful*," she murmured huskily.

His throat went so dry that he couldn't respond, which didn't seem to bother Ariel. Fully awake now— far too awake for his peace of mind—she promptly scooted on top of him, completely insensitive to the sudden lung-crushing weight on his chest. Instinctively he anchored her there more securely, so she wouldn't fall off.

The weight and intimate feel of her soft, sleek body aroused him all over again. When she lifted her head, he could see those sleepy eyes were full of sass, her mouth butter-soft and temptingly curved in the smug, feline smile of a cream-sated cat. He stroked her bottom lip, dismally aware that he couldn't keep his hands off her and didn't have even an ounce of willpower to try.

"You feel wonderful, too," she informed him.

"You think so?"

"I know so. I wore you out, Josh."

"You destroyed me," he tactfully corrected her. Her response was a grin. A wicked, feminine, delighted grin. For the fifth time in five minutes, he thought man, she was trouble.

"I'll take some of the blame, but you get the lion's share. You knocked my socks off, Penoyer. I'm a grown woman and I could have sworn I knew what's what. You blew that one out of the water, and frankly, I'm resentful. I'm not used to having my socks knocked off."

He lifted the sheet and gravely peeked over her shoulder. "Looks to me like you lost a whole lot more than your socks."

A merciless finger scraped down his side, tickling his ribs, forcing a chuckle from him. When she refused to quit tickling, he was justifiably forced to pin her beneath him and kiss her. And then she forced—downright forced him—to kiss her again, because her mouth was irresistibly sweet and her arms wrapped so willingly around him.

Maybe he could have resisted harder if he wasn't so inadequate with words. She'd known what to say to make his lover's ego soar like an eagle, but his tongue tripped and tied around intimate talk. He wanted her to know, needed her to know, that she was unforgettable and special, that she was giving and loving beyond any fantasy of a lover he'd ever dreamed of. No words were going to cut the mustard. Nothing ever came out of his mouth right, not with a woman, never with her, so the best he could do was indelibly show her how he felt.

"Josh?"

"Hmm?"

"We should stop."

"I know." And he really did know. Falling in love with her was mistake enough; making love with her again was as foolhardy as a nosedive into quicksand. She was never the free spirit she portrayed. She was vulnerable as hell, which he knew intimately well now. Ariel had reason to be wary of commitment, reason to avoid men who were proven failures at happily-everafters—like him. Only, when he studied her face, her cheeks were flushed and her voice was hoarse and those eyes—there was just no way he could ignore the naked-soft desire in those eyes.

"I think I only had one of those little packets in the drawer—"

"I know." The lack of condoms should have sparked a jolt of sanity, but that didn't work, either. There were other ways to please her, other ways to make love. He could think of a half dozen he'd like to test on her, with her, for her.

"And I'm not sure what time your kids are expecting you home, but something tells me you never planned to be out this late—"

Guilt bolted through Josh when she mentioned the children. He never forgot his kids. They were his life. It was a disturbing, unnerving sensation to discover that he hadn't thought about his kids, his responsibilities, his whole normal life—even once—since the moment he'd walked through her door.

He opened his mouth to answer her, when abruptly, the telephone jangled by her bedside, startling both of them.

Ariel glanced swiftly at the clock, then at him. "I'd better answer it. Your kids know you're here, don't they? So it could be them. I don't know anyone else who would be calling this late—"

He nodded in agreement, and eased away from that too-tempting embrace so she could lift up and reach the phone. Before the third ring, she'd grabbed the receiver.

His body was still charged with desire; the crazy spell she wove around him was still jet-hammering through his pulse. Even so, he was half braced to grab his clothes. As she'd guessed, his kids knew where he was, and the only reason he could imagine anyone telephoning this late was trouble. Maybe Killer had another nightmare. Or something had broken. Or someone was hurt. In those few seconds, Josh was so sure it must be Calvin calling that he never expected to hear her say, "Mason? What's wrong?"

Mason.

Her old live-in boyfriend.

"No, I can't really talk right now...."

Ice shot through his veins, where seconds before there'd been fire. He switched on the bedside lamp. At some point after the storm, the electric power must have been restored, because the lamp worked ... and the light instantly pooled in a pale glow on her face. She was holding the receiver tight to her ear, but looking at him. No way to miss how suddenly nervous she was—her eyes were luminous, her hands unsteady as she fretfully pushed the hair off her face. "It's all right, Mason. Of course I understand. I just..."

Like a fuse suddenly unplugged in his brain, Josh stopped listening. He swung over the opposite side of the bed and started searching for his clothes. They seemed to be strewn from one end of her apartment to the other, reminding him—painfully—of exactly how wild and fast and explosively they'd come together.

Once he'd yanked on jeans, he found his shoes in the hall, his belt and shirt around the kitchen. His mind spun a chain link of a hundred thoughts, and every one of them was a harsh, blunt reality check.

At midnight, old boyfriends felt free to call her. For some confounded reason, he'd actually started to believe that what he felt for her—what they were together—was unique, special, powerfully rare. But that phone call underlined what he had no business forgetting. She'd had lovers before, relationships before, that undoubtedly had been unique and special to her. If none of those had tempted her toward commitment, he'd have to be dead drunk to believe she'd be tempted by a guy with a ready-made family of hellions and a divorce smudge in his personal history.

Josh thought, *I have to be crazy to be here.*

Dressed, truck keys already clutched in his fist, he headed back for the bedroom. She was just hanging up the phone. "You were right," he said swiftly. "It's late, and the kids weren't expecting me to be gone this long. I need to head home."

If she heard the comment, it didn't seem to register. She went suddenly still, her face fragile and white as she looked at him. "You're... upset with me."

Josh expelled a harsh breath. "No, I'm upset with me. We don't play by the same rules, Ariel, which I sure as hell knew before this. But somehow I thought... damn, I don't know what I thought. But if you're getting calls from old lovers in the middle of the night, your idea of what's kosher and mine aren't even in the same ballpark."

She drew up her legs, as if suddenly realizing she was bare, and wrapped her arms around them tight. "Josh, I'm not still having a relationship with this man. It's been over for more than two years—"

"You must have left a few ends dangling, if he feels free to call you at any hour of the night—" He caught himself up sharp, aware his temper was skittering on a razor edge. He wanted to fight with her. Too damn much. He wanted to tear away that emerald-green

sheet and make love to her until she forgot every ex-
lover she'd ever had. Too damn much.

He forced the slam-beat of his pulse to slow down.
"I'm sorry," he said gruffly. "That comment was out
of line. Who you keep friends with is your business."
The truck key dug into his clenched palm. "But I really do have to leave. Not because of that phone call
or anything like that. If the kids woke up and found
me gone, they wouldn't know what's what."

"I understand," she said softly, and took a long
careful breath. "You're regretting it, aren't you...our
making love?"

She didn't phrase it like a question, but she just sat
there with her arms wrapped around her knees, her
hair tumbling over her shoulders, the expression in her
eyes as fragile as bone china. His response was rough
and swift. "If hell froze over, I couldn't regret making love with you. I'll never regret making love with
you. But dammit, Ariel..."

When words failed him, she quietly filled in the
blanks. "But you don't want it to happen again. Your
kids...they've already gotten too many ideas about
the two of us. You don't want them hurt by building
up unrealistic expectations. And an affair, an intimate relationship—we'd never be able to pull that off
without the children guessing what was going on."

Shortly after that, Josh let himself out her back
door and barreled down the back alley stairs. Striding
toward his Bronco, he told himself he felt relief—
enormous relief—at Ariel's perception and sensitiv-
ity. Snapping off a relationship right after making
love, she could have been mad. She could have been
hurt. Instead, she'd just honestly seemed to understand that he had an insolvable problem.

There was no way he could pull off an intimate affair with his kids around. Especially his sons. Teenage boys *always* had sex on their minds. If he tried staying out all night, Cal and Bruiser would guess in a blink that he was sleeping with Ariel. That couldn't happen. He was the kids' role model, their strongest moral influence. A good father sure as hell didn't conduct a sexual affair in front of his kids, and a good man never let emotions overrule his common sense. How could he teach those values without living up to them as an example?

He jumped into the truck and plugged in the key. For a moment, though, instead of turning on the engine, he stared blindly in the darkness. The rain-washed night was cool, dark and as silent as loneliness.

He had no choice, he repeated to himself. Marriage wasn't even a line item on Ariel's dance card. Especially not marriage to him. Unless the lady could be coaxed into believing in commitment, his kids—his whole life—made a relationship impossible to pursue. That was no headliner.

Making love to her had been a headliner, though. The acid churning in his stomach, the raw taste in the back of his throat—those were news items, too. He'd never let emotions rule his behavior before, but nothing mattered to him in the past few hours—not his kids, not his life, not reality. Just her.

He didn't want to leave her. He didn't want to let her go, not tonight, not any night—not ever—and it stung like the bite of a whip to diminish their lovemaking into a one-night stand. That wasn't what he felt for her. It wasn't what he wanted for her. No woman, ever, had wrapped a clenched fist around his heart the way she did.

Josh turned the key and listened to the engine come alive with a throaty roar. He'd never denied fear, had always owned up to—and faced—the things he was scared of in life. But he couldn't remember being afraid like this. Afraid, shook up and feeling scissor-edged angry—with himself. They had no future. Why was it so hard to get that through his head?

A grown man knew better than to play with dynamite. He simply *had* to stay away from her.

Ariel dipped a spoon in the pint of butter-brickle ice cream, with her gaze focused on the necklace on her worktable. Dot was out front with the customers. There weren't many, not since the afternoon had turned swelteringly humid and sticky hot.

The problematic necklace wasn't an antique, just a reproduction. The jewelry had been copied from a piece Greer Garson wore for the movie *Pride and Prejudice*. In the original, the wreath of diamonds was designed to look like nineteenth-century lace. It was a stunning piece, although the reproduction, of course, had rhinestones instead of diamonds. The problem, Ariel mused, was that there were rhinestones—and then there were rhinestones. It was one thing to fool a crowd, and another to fool yourself. These stones looked too damned fake, and they were ruining the piece.

She scooped out another spoonful of butter brickle, letting the ice cream melt on her tongue, frowning. All the rhinestones didn't need replacing. Just the cheapos. Which would easily improve the looks and value of the piece, if she'd just move her fanny and *do* it.

Instead, she was halfway through the pint of butter brickle and her mind was consumingly focused. Just not on work.

Josh hadn't called in three days—which was fine, just *fine,* by her. A thick driblet of ice cream plopped on her thigh. Exasperated, she carried the pint to the sink, wiped the carton and shelved it back in the minifreezer. She'd had enough ice cream. She'd had enough of being miserable about Josh, too.

Their night together had been the stuff of dreams until Mason telephoned. Mason, the doofus, had been too excited to realize how late he was calling her. Suzanna, the woman he'd been involved with, had agreed to accept his ring and he just wanted to share the engagement news. Ariel could easily have explained that to Josh—if he'd given her the chance. He hadn't. Not only did the cretin have an antiquated possessive streak, but he'd never even *tried* to listen, for which she'd been mightily tempted to strangle him.

There wasn't an ounce of violence in her nature. She wasn't the strangling type. And she'd never been scissor-edged restless and miserable over a man. There was never any reason to be. She'd always handled the men in her life carefully, tactfully, honestly. She never fought. She never made herself sick, bingeing on butter-brickle ice cream. She'd never done anything with a man that made her feel ashamed or uneasy—until Josh.

She'd fallen for him, fallen drowning-deep and keening-hard. Love, though, was no excuse for selfishness. She wasn't a practical realist like him; she often let emotions overrule her actions—but never when someone could potentially be hurt. He had three very hurt and vulnerable children. He needed a mom for those kids, not just a lover for himself. She had to be the least qualified and most inadequate woman on the planet to be a mom—which, dammit, she'd known before making love with him.

Everything about her relationship with Josh was all wrong and dangerous and, positively, seeing him again would be a mistake. Seeing any of the Penoyers again was a sure route to heartache. It was a relief he hadn't called. A total and complete relief. A *wonderful* relief.

"Ariel?" Dot's head poked around the office doorway. "I think I've got something to cheer you up."

"I don't need cheering up." For a brief, extremely brief, millisecond, her mind had flashed on the Technicolor memory of their making love. His naked body, illuminated in a wash of lightning. The intense storm of fire in his eyes. The sweep of his hands down her flesh, the terrifyingly elemental feeling of vulnerability, his cherishing kisses that only made her feel more vulnerable, more awake, more alive as a woman than she'd even known was possible. Ariel yanked a strand of hair off her brow, willing that upsetting, unsettling memory to the trash heap. "I don't need cheering up," she snapped to Dot again.

Dot raised her arms in a surrender gesture. "I'm not going to argue with you, Ms. Grump. I was just trying to tell you that you had a visitor."

"Who?" But tarnation. She could already see who. The pipsqueak wearing the backward baseball cap was peeking around Dot's hip, making Ariel's heart sink faster than a fat chunk of lead. She'd rather face a gang of thugs in a dark alley than any Penoyer right now and, oh God, especially not the squirt. Her callously insensitive partner winked, then mercilessly turned on her heel and left them alone.

"Hi, Ariel," Killer said cautiously. "Are you in a bad mood? Too bad a mood to wanna see me?"

"Of course not, love bug. I'm always glad to see you." The lie would have made a con artist proud, but one glance at the child and Ariel banished her own problems. Something was wrong. Real wrong. Killer's plain face was blotchy, her eyes brimming with anxiety and nervousness. "Come on in. Take a stool up here by me.... You want a soda pop?"

"Orange."

Ariel fetched it, exasperatingly aware that she'd started stocking that particular flavor of soft drink solely because it was the urchin's favorite. She popped the lid before handing it over. "What's up, sweets?"

"Nothin's up. Everything's awful. Dad's mad. At me." Killer guzzled a swig of the pop and wiped her mouth with the back of her hand. "I always forgot how much I hate it when he's mad at me."

Keep your mouth shut, Ariel cautioned herself. *Nothing about the Penoyer family is any of your business. You have to quit caring and keep your nose out.* It was superb advice. But how the Sam Hill was she supposed to ignore those woebegone eyes? "I don't suppose there's some reason why he's mad at you?" she asked delicately.

"Oh, yeah, there's a reason. Mom came over to pick me up. She was supposed to be taking all us kids out to dinner. Only, I locked myself in the bathroom until she was gone, and Dad...he was real mad. He said Mom loved me and I was acting like a real brat and enough was enough." Her tone was a morose mimic of her dad's. She sighed heavily and long. "Ariel . . . can I tell you something?"

Ariel sank on the adjoining metal stool and braced her chin in the wedge of her palm. The only intelligent, safe answer she could give the child was no. The instant Patrice mentioned her mother, Ariel recognized she was over her head—this was Josh's private business, nothing she had any right to touch. Yet the child was looking at her, waiting, expectant. And with a feeling of doom and gloom, she heard herself saying, "Sure, sweetheart."

"I saw Nancy kissing this guy," Killer promptly blurted out.

"Nancy? You mean your mom?"

Killer nodded and gulped another slug of pop. It swallowed easier, now that the momentous confession was out. "The guy was there when I got home from preschool a coupla times. Once I came home from playing at Jonesey's 'cause Jonesey got sick. Only, the door was locked and I was scared 'cause I couldn't get in. He was there that time, too. The boys don't know about him. And neither does my dad. So you *can't* tell, Ariel, okay?"

"Honey . . ." Who could have guessed that a full-blown peptic ulcer could come on this quick?

"Next thing I know, she's outa there. She told my dad she was stuffled. She told him we kids were driving her crazy and he never 'preciated her. She made my dad feel awful. I know, 'cause I found him crying all by himself one time and my dad, he don't cry, not ever, no way. She told him all this stuff to make him feel bad, but she never told him about this guy. Ariel, you got any ice cream?"

It seemed a daunting measure of her kinship with the child that they were on the same wavelength about comfort foods in times of trauma. "Butter brickle. And I think we need marshmallows and cherries on top, don't you?"

"I'd say two cherries," Killer said gravely.

"No problem. A two-cherry sundae coming right up." Ariel pushed up off the stool. There wasn't much left in the pint carton, but enough to create a masterpiece of a minisundae in a coffee mug. No reason to make two; her appetite—even for butter brickle—had disappeared the second this conversation started. And though she made the most sinfully diverting minisundae in her considerable repertoire, it didn't stop Killer from talking.

"Nancy wants me to go to her place sometimes. But I did that, at first. Dad'd take me to the door and take me in...but when he left, Mr. Nerdo was there. I don't like him. She divorced us. I don't see why I gotta see him, and, Ariel, I gotta ask you something—"

"Just a second, honey." Ariel had ignored the sound of the telephone ringing, but Dot showed back up in the doorway holding the receiver. "I don't care if a nuclear war was just declared. I'm not here," she said to Dot.

"I kind of guessed that, but I wasn't sure. Gotcha." Dot disappeared again.

"Now..." Ariel grabbed some napkins. Clearly Patrice considered eating sundaes to be a whole-body experience. Drools and driblets of ice cream were flying everywhere. "What did you want to ask me?"

"I thought maybe you could fix it with my dad about his being mad at me. I know you could do it. Only reason Nancy wanted to see me was to tell me

how much fun school was gonna be. *Everybody's*
trying to talk to me about that. They must think I'm
stupid. And it's not like I'd believe *her* about anything anymore. So if you could just talk to my dad…''
Killer waved her spoon expressively. ''But you *can't*
tell him about the jerk. And there was another thing I
had to ask you, Ariel. You don't need insurance, do
you?''

''Insurance?'' Ariel asked blankly, confused how
the word had ever entered the conversation.

''The jerk. That's what he was doing. Selling Nancy
insurance all those times. I asked my dad what insurance was. He said it was something you had to have
and was a pain to pay for, but nothing I had to worry
about. But I'm worried. *You* don't need insurance, do
you?''

''No, honey.''

''Because I don't think it's fair. I don't think you
should leave your whole family and divorce everybody like they're nothing—not for something stupid
like insurance.''

Ariel pressed a palm on her abdomen, but it didn't
stop her stomach from churning acid. She refused to
feel guilty about letting the child talk. The weight of
this secret about Mr. Nerdo had obviously preyed on
Patrice's mind, and it had to be better for the child to
get the problem off her chest—only Ariel never anticipated the mountain of stress suddenly pressing on her
own.

She had no idea if Josh knew this guy had been in
the wings when his wife left him. If not, she'd rather
chew rats than be the one who spilled those particular
beans. Worse yet, this whole problem painfully underlined why she didn't belong in Josh's life. His

daughter had come to her, seeking mom-type advice. She felt as inadequate as an Eskimo floundering in the tropics. How could she possibly cope as a substitute mom, when she had no clue what to say to Killer, no idea what a real mom would do in her shoes?

And that small pair of unforgettable chocolate-brown eyes were peeled right on her face, less-than-patiently waiting for her to say *something.* "I agree with you, love bug," she said carefully. "Nothing about a divorce is fair—especially for the kids. But I'm afraid even big people can't always escape making mistakes. They don't mean to, but even grown-ups don't always have good judgment—"

"I think you got great jud'ment. You like my dad, don't you? And you like me?"

Ariel swallowed. She didn't need a thwack with a baseball bat to realize where the child was heading. "Killer, you need to listen to me. Your dad and I like each other fine, but we're not getting married. I *know* you've had that idea on your mind, but it just isn't going to happen, honey. Life just can't be as simple as you want it to be—"

"I think if you keep insurance out of it, it could be a lot simpler."

Fifty years from now, Ariel told herself she was going to laugh about parts of this conversation. She was entirely in agreement with the six-year-old's philosophy about fidelity—and life. But just then, she had no time to smile. The child had started this whole impossible visit with a question, and she couldn't avoid answering it forever.

"I know you asked me to talk to your dad," she said gently, "but I think you're the one who needs to do that, Patrice. And I want you to know something.

There's nothing that you have to be afraid to tell your dad, whether it's about that guy or anything else. Your dad wants to know when something's bothering you—it's the only way he can help. And he's an adult, honey. You don't have to worry that he can't handle things, because he can."

Killer considered this, then shook her curly head. "You don't know how sad he was. It took forever before he was yelling at us and playing with us and being with us like it used to be. I don't want him sad like he was. Ever again."

"I understand. But this is different, love bug. I think he knows something's worrying you. I really think he'd feel better, not worse, if he knew what it was. And I think it'd make you feel better, too."

Killer eventually agreed to have that conversation with Josh, and the urchin left a few minutes later. Once alone, Ariel sat and pressed the heels of her hands against her eyes. Her conscience was dredging guilt, sure she'd handled that badly. Josh had a right and need to know anything that troubled his daughter, but Mr. Nerdo had to be a hurtful, touchy subject for him—and her interference involving such a personal problem had to be as welcome as a skunk.

There was a chance, of course, that Patrice would talk to Josh without her name ever entering into the conversation. With just a little luck, the problem could be resolved without Josh ever knowing that she'd been involved....

"Ariel? You okay?"

Ariel lifted her head, just then aware that Dot had wandered in the back room to filch a soda. Her partner's eyes were far too shrewd to pull off a lie. "No.

But I'll get over it. I know I've been a pistol to get along with for the past few days. I'm sorry, Dot.''

"Hey, no sweat. How many times have you been there for me when I had a problem? I'd just hoped the visit from that little ragamuffin would cheer you up. I know you're fond of her—"

"I love her," Ariel admitted.

"Yeah, I had that feeling."

"Every time I see her—every damn time—she gives me ulcers and she worries me and she ties me up in knots. But I swear I couldn't love that child more if she were my own."

"I had that feeling, too, hon."

"Well, I'm just going to have to forget her. And her brothers. And for double damn sure, I have to forget their dad," Ariel said resolutely.

"If that's what you have to do—"

"It is," she said firmly. She pushed up off the stool, thinking it was time she put her life back in order, time she got some work done, time every waking moment wasn't immersed on the Penoyers.

But then her gaze fell absently on the worktable.

The necklace she'd been working on, the Greer Garson repro, had disappeared.

Ten

___

Well, his kleptomaniac kid had struck again. Josh lifted the heavy weight of the necklace in his hands. No moonlight reached the back alley, at least where he was hunched on the metal stairs by her back door. Still the stones shimmered like water in the shadows, dancing diamonds and sparks of light.

A car door slammed below.

Instinctively he braced, although Ariel had left no lights on and she clearly hadn't spotted him yet. God knew where she'd been. It was just past ten, the night a pitchy-witchy black and hot, the trees still as ghosts in the airless shadows.

She bent down to grab her purse and some kind of unwieldly-size tapestry tote bag, and then he heard her heels clicking on the pavement. He tightened his hold on the necklace until the stones bit into his palm.

Man, was she dressed to prowl. All in black, a jumpsuit that struck him as appropriate for a cat burglar—or a woman single-mindedly determined to drive a man crazy. The fabric tucked just so around her fanny, draped high on her throat, palmed her breasts with a lover's possessiveness. Her hair lit up the night, flowing down her back in a free-fall of silver-gold.

When she reached the step, she glanced up. And stopped dead. "Josh—!"

"I didn't mean to scare you. I was just hoping to catch you home. It seems I have something that belongs to you that needs returning."

"Oh, God. You found the necklace."

"A little hard to miss. When I first saw it on her dresser, I thought hell, Killer's moved into the felony league. These stones look like a Tiffany bankroll. I almost had a stroke, I was that scared they were real—"

"They're just rhinestones." A feather of a smile but her eyes hadn't left his face yet.

Whether he was welcome, he wasn't sure. But he was sure he'd missed her. He was sure—damn sure—that no woman had ever looked at him the way she did . . . the way she was looking at him now. All those nerves in her eyes. All that emotion. For him.

God knew how he'd believed he could give her up. He'd never find an Ariel again. There was no other Ariel, no woman remotely, uniquely like her—but he'd shut her down and run after their last encounter. Could be she had some damn good reasons not to give him a second chance, and temporarily, he was grateful for his pint-size thief of a daughter. If Killer hadn't provided unfinished business, he wasn't positive Ariel would let him in the door.

Hesitantly she climbed the stairs, juggling her tote bag and purse to fish for her apartment key. Her eyes flashed at him nervously, then ducked back to her purse. "I must look like I'm dressed pretty weird, like for Halloween or something. It's just an outfit I wear when I'm doing magic. Every second Thursday night, I put on a little show—do some magic tricks—at a nursing home. One of my family's there. Harry. He's my dad's older brother's second wife's uncle. Anyway—"

"You don't look weird. You look great. And you don't have to explain about the family relationship." It was one of the things that occurred to him when he'd been staring at the ceiling at three in the morning. He'd misunderstood Ariel's feeling for family. Pinning down her convoluted kinship relationships defied all sanity, but he'd somehow missed that telling detail—she'd literally created family in order to have one. She stood by the people she loved no differently than he did.

She plugged the key in the lock and pushed open the back door, but no way she was in any hurry to let him in. "It's awfully late. If all you want is to return the necklace—"

"I won't stay long. But I'd like to talk to you for a minute about Patrice." As he'd expected, his daughter's problems got him in—nothing else. But for that tug of an instant when he stepped closer, he was near enough to see her wary green eyes, to have wrapped her hair around a hand and made those wary green eyes close, maybe, if he kissed her right. If he kissed the way he wanted to.

Possibly she guessed his intentions, because she jogged past him quicker than a frisky colt. It was dark inside and close, as if all the night heat and humidity had concentrated in her kitchen. In the distance he could hear the susurrant drone of an air conditioner from behind her closed bedroom door. She kicked off her heels, lowering her height two inches, then flicked on the sink light and aimed for the fridge.

Faster than a speeding bullet, she flipped the lid on a beer and handed it to him. Poor baby. Not much question that she was hoping he'd chug it and split. He took a sip—a small one—from the steaming-cold can, but only because his throat was so dry.

"You talked to Killer. I owe you a serious thanks. Since the divorce, my ex-wife hasn't exactly been trying to make a secret out of her...uh...sidekick. But I had no idea her relationship with the guy was bothering Patrice. Maybe it'd have never come out if you hadn't coaxed her into talking to me."

She plopped the tapestry bag on the table, and was pulling things out—first, a crystal ball that made jewel colors flash on the ceiling and walls. Then a witch's wand. And then a pile of rainbow-hued scarves that apparently required immediate folding, because she was sure suddenly unbelievably busy, fussing with those scarves. "I was afraid...that you'd be angry with me for interfering."

"I could have sworn we'd already been through this road. Sweet pea, you get the strangest ideas about what would make me mad." He shook his head. "Stuff like that belongs out in the open. Finally Patrice's behavior, her acting out and especially with her mother, makes a lot more sense. No way to deal with a problem that's hidden in a closet."

Amazing, how much time it was taking her to fold a few silk scarves. "So..." she said carefully, "it sounds as if you already knew about this guy."

"Paul? Sure I knew about him." He moved closer, set his beer on the table. "He was hitting on my ex-wife long before the divorce. I never told the kids. Maybe hiding it like a secret was a mistake, but I didn't want them thinking something bad about their mother. She's screwing up. Paul's good-looking, with lots of charisma, but the guy is a real jerk with a long history of chasing skirts and taking women for a ride."

She said nothing for a moment, but she finally forgot those damn scarves and looked at him. Something was in her eyes—the strangest expression of both confusion and relief. It took him a second to make any sense of it. "You thought I'd be hurt, if I had to talk about this guy with Killer?" he asked.

She nodded.

Josh groped for a way to explain. "Her cheating on me ripped real sharp for a while—can't deny that. But this guy is nobody I respect, so it wasn't exactly the same as feeling jealous. If Paul sparked her engines, we definitely had nothing left to say to each other. I not only couldn't be like him, I didn't want to be like him. Can you understand?"

She nodded again.

"So have we cleared that up? He's not my favorite subject in town, but I'm not gonna be hurt if he shows up in a conversation. And I wouldn't give a damn if I *was* hurt. I don't want forbidden waters between us. If you want to know something, ask, okay?"

"Okay."

That "okay" was a borderline fib, Josh thought. He was still watching her eyes. There were shadows in those forest-green woods, something he was still missing. "Maybe we've got another deck that needs clearing here? You thought I'd be upset if I had to talk about Paul . . . and you also thought I'd be mad—because you bent over backward to give time and attention and damned good advice to my daughter?"

"I wasn't sure it was good advice, Josh."

"Sure seemed like the brilliant brand to me. Nobody got that problem out of her, except for you."

There. Finally it came out—honesty—and pouring faster than spilled milk. "You could have resented me for interfering, especially on something as delicate and tough as this. I don't know anything about families. Except for the dysfunctional kind. So you could have thought it was real presumptuous of me to ever give advice to your kids, especially to Killer."

He'd heard that song tune before, but in a flash of insight, he realized he should have listened more closely to the lyrics. All this time, the confounded woman had led him to believe she was antimarriage, anti all the commitments that came with marriage and kids. But being scared wasn't the same thing as being against. How was he supposed to guess she was carrying around a heartful of insecurities about parenting?

That rare flash of insight was important, Josh sensed. Only damned if he knew what to do about it. "No way you did anything 'presumptuous' in my book," he said carefully. "You know about divorce, so who'd know more about what my kids are feeling than you? And hell, Ariel. My monsters confuse me five times before Sunday on a good week. Parenting doesn't come up with a rule book. No matter what background you bring to the job, I don't think anyone feels prepared or qualified—"

"Josh?"

"Yeah?"

"If I'd said the right thing to her," Ariel said quietly, "she wouldn't have stolen the necklace."

The necklace. He'd meant to immediately return the jewelry, yet for some strange reason, he discovered it still clutched in his hand. Maybe that was no real surprise. For over an hour, sitting on her back steps in the dark, he'd sifted the trinket of stones through his fingers, watching them catch light and fire where there should have been no light or fire, thinking, dammit, they were just like her.

Jewels were alien to his life. Not only were they an expense he couldn't afford, but he was always afraid of breaking fragile, delicate chains with his calloused hands and rough ways. He'd never denied his need for a woman. He'd just thought that when his kids were grown, when his life was back in order, when he had the time, he'd go looking again. Only, Ariel had most inconveniently barreled into his life now, with her whimsical magic and her sensual allure and the nasty way she had of turning every day lighter, brighter— damn near dazzling brighter—whenever she was around. And telling himself that a sensual, vulnerable jewel didn't belong in his life wasn't working worth spit.

It seemed his youngest monster had figured that out ahead of him. Josh didn't need a whomp upside the head to realize why Patrice had become light-fingered around Ariel. Her stealing trinkets forced the two of them together, but he couldn't count on the squirt's tricks to work forever. She was just a baby.

Grand larceny—absconding with a serious jewel— was definitely a man's job. Never mind what the risks were; losing her would be like losing his own heart-beat. Knowing Ariel's skittishness around marriage, Josh didn't doubt that she could disappear from his life as fast as she'd barreled into it... unless he did something to fight for her.

He lifted the necklace to the light, glanced at the clasp and then at the snuggle-high neckline of Ariel's outfit. Her eyebrows arched curiously when he leaned forward, but she stood stock-still when he lifted her hair and attached the clasp behind her neck.

"What on earth are you—?"

"I just wondered how it would look on you. Maybe they're rhinestones, but they look like diamonds to me. And I can imagine you walking into a party wearing something like this, elegant, classy, so expensive you look forbidden to every guy in the place—although you being you, I doubt you'd even guess why you were drawing every man's eye...."

He stepped back and cocked his head, as if he were studying the effect of the necklace against the stark black fabric. A soft peach flush climbed her cheeks. Her hand had shot up to touch the necklace, her fingers not quite steady and her eyes not quite steady, either, flickering on his with the sudden restless, fragile flush of nerves. Feminine nerves. Electric nerves.

"Naw," he said abruptly. "Something's wrong. It doesn't look right at all."

"Josh, for heaven's sake." She chuckled, but the sound came out thready and not like her voice at all. "Of course it doesn't look right. It's formal jewelry and I'm just wearing a jumpsuit, and believe me, I'd never be wearing anything like this unless it was for fun—"

Gently he cut her off. "You're right. It's the jump-suit that makes it look wrong. Against the black, it's real pretty and all, but I'm almost positive it'd look better next to bare skin. At least your bare skin."

The pulse leapt in her throat when he leaned for-ward again. She said, "Josh, I don't know what you're...." when he swished aside a swath of her hair again, encouraged her chin to rest on his shoulder and reached for the zipper in back.

She said, "Josh, I don't know..." when she heard the slinky metallic sound of the zipper sliding down, down past the wisp of a bra strap to the hollow of her spine.

And then she just said, "Josh," real thick, when he chased all that silly, unnecessary fabric down her shoulders and arms, freeing the necklace to drop, in a dash and splash of light, on her bare throat.

It was hot in the kitchen. Real hot, and sticky-sultry humid, so there was no logical reason for her to shiver, even if she was uncovered to the waist except for a satin snippet of a bra. The bra was sin black and looked like a torture device to Josh. Some sadistic de-signer had engineered the thing with a man-chal-lenging front clasp and supporting wires. Probably a woman. Only a woman would do that to another woman, make her think that she needed to be pushed up and out instead of knowing—as any man did—that natural was better. Natural was *always* better.

Josh didn't want her to be uncomfortable.

So he flipped the front catch.

Her breasts spilled free, escaping that imprisoning confinement as if they'd been dying for freedom, looking white in the shadowy light, looking firm and full and as naturally exquisite as he remembered. Ariel's lips parted. She tried to say something—maybe his name again—but nothing came out. She seemed to be having trouble breathing.

So was he.

"I had a feeling that might make the difference," he said. "Now the necklace looks just right."

"Josh—"

"Hmm?"

"You're not... looking at the necklace."

Of course he wasn't looking at the necklace. He didn't give a holy patootie damn about the necklace.

"And somehow I don't think you have jewelry on your mind—"

She was, always had been, he'd noticed, an extraordinarily perceptive woman. And sensitive. Terrifyingly sensitive, when he nipped the side of her long white throat just so. She shivered again. Shivered hard this time.

Her hands had shot down to grab her jumpsuit before it fell down completely. That cause was abandoned when he claimed her hands and wrapped them around his neck. By the time he lifted her on the table and stepped between her thighs, the jumpsuit had shivered the rest of the way down and dropped in a puddle of fabric on the floor. He was kissing her by then, his mouth fused on hers like the perfect fit between prong and socket. Electricity was his business. He knew all about prongs and sockets, but damned if he understood the fire of short circuits she aroused in him.

Want seared through him, hotter than a fresh burn. Need made his blood rush loud, roaring in his ears like a tiger that wouldn't be ignored. Lord. He never planned this, never expected that impulsively putting that dang fool necklace on her would turn into this.

Or maybe he had. Maybe he'd have done just about anything to remind her what happened between them. And it had been this way with her, right from the start. A tornado wind, coming at him from nowhere. An avalanche, erupting on a sun-soft peaceful day. Magic—and never mind if he'd never believed in anything frivolous or foolhardy—because the spell his lady wove around him was as real as time. And a thousand times more precious.

His hand grappled behind her and groped blind for the round hard shape of the crystal ball. It was in the way. He cupped the weight of it, and without opening his eyes, found a home on a kitchen chair to stash it. The table was hardly a comfortable mattress, but traveling the five miles to her bedroom was an untenable option. The fire was happening here and now, and he was afraid to leave the blaze untended for even seconds. Ariel wasn't exactly communicating patience.

She pushed and pulled at his shirt buttons until they were free. Her hands felt small and damp-hot on his bare skin, clutching his shoulders, winding around his back and neck. Her lips were still fused with his, but those first sweet-slow, drowning-soft kisses had turned into a restless rage of kisses, wild and urgent and greedy. Greed for him—if he could believe it.

Her fingers reached down to tangle and battle with his belt buckle. He slipped off her scrap of panties, then dug in his back pocket for a condom before shagging off the rest of his clothes. Protecting her was the last coherent thought he had. Somewhere he heard the scream of a distant siren, the baby hum of a muffled air conditioner, the hiss of a car passing. None of those life sounds were real. The only real thing on the whole planet was her, and the dynamite rush of singing, stinging emotion he felt for her... that he hoped he could make her feel for him.

He wrapped her legs around his waist and took her, watching her eyes, watching the taut strain build in her face, until he was impaled in her, deep and completely. He slowed everything down then. Way down. The rush was too damn delicious to waste on speed, and this wasn't about speed. It was about tenderness on fire.

He laid his lover back on the bed of rainbow-hued scarves. The silk looked rich against her pale skin. The stones of the necklace glowed and glittered with every rasping breath she took, but neither silk nor jewels competed with her. Her flesh was lush, as sweat-slick as his own, her eyes fierce and soul-bare with emotion.

She loved him. He knew it. Felt it in her shuddering kisses, saw it in her uninhibited vulnerability, sensed it in the treasuring way she touched him. This didn't have a damn thing to do with sex, and never mind that he was hot enough to steam the Arctic. He'd made love before. It was never like this. She couldn't give herself to him, not like this, unless that terrifying emotion of love was part of the connection.

The shaggy bear of terror stuck its claws in him, too. Passion alone never won a woman. He was no hero, just a mistake-ridden ordinary man, and his failed marriage made him a shaky investment for a woman who was already afraid of believing in futures. He couldn't give her guarantees. Life came with none.

All he could do was promise her what love meant—what two people could build and create together—and with that on his mind, with nothing else in his heart, he did his best to burn up the night. For her. With her.

Josh wasn't exactly sure how they ended up in her bed. He vaguely remembered feeling guilty—a wild tryst on a kitchen table was no way to treat a lady—so that was the motivation behind the move. Something had malfunctioned in his conscience system, though, because he hadn't exactly been successful in treating her like a lady in her cool, quiet, air-conditioned bedroom, either. This ceaseless hunger for her had become an embarrassing problem. The only solution he could think of was making love to her every night for the next three, four thousand years.

But Ariel hadn't necessarily reached that same conclusion.

She was awake. So was he—wasted, but awake—and the hour was past two. His kids were surely asleep and they had her phone number if there was a problem, but he didn't want them waking in the morning to a missing dad. Soon he'd have to oust himself from her bed and go home. But not yet.

Just then, he was painfully conscious that she'd barely said a word throughout their whole wild night. She'd never murmured even a token ''no,'' and her willingness to make love had been unmistakably, unforgettably clear. Still, her silence was vastly different from a spoken ''Yes,'' or a spoken ''I love you,'' or a nice, clean-cut ''Josh Penoyer, I want you in my future.''

And her silence was starting to scare him, partly because she was unquestionably awake. Her eyes were wide-open and focused, softer than silk, on his face. Hours ago he'd removed the unwieldy sparkler of a necklace. She was as naked as a woman could be, her cheek creased on the pillow next to his, her long hair tumbling all over the place and her mouth looking swollen and well kissed. But her face looked pale as pride in the moonlight. And he'd understood what she wanted when her eyes looked all smoky and dazed, but her eyes were forest black and clear right now. She was thinking.

Ariel could come up with some confounded crazy ideas when she started thinking.

"Are we...feeling okay?" he tried, and won a wisp of a smile.

"We are feeling splendiforous."

That was good. Real good, he told himself. Only, not quite enough. Ariel had this diverting gift for making him feel sky-high as a lover and a man. How she was feeling was a lot harder for her to put on the table.

"Are we conceivably...upset about anything?"

"Nope."

"Are we, maybe, mad about anything? Mad, hurt, worried, annoyed—"

She cut him off with the softest of whispers. "I don't understand what you do to me, Josh."

"Are we talking about making love on the kitchen table? Hell, I know I didn't get my boots off. I never meant to come at you like some kind of animal, I swear. I just didn't expect—"

"Neither did I. And I loved making love on the kitchen table. The place, the speed, the rush—I'll never forget this night as long as I live. Don't you dare apologize for anything, Penoyer. It's just...nothing like that ever happened to me before. And every time I'm with you, I seem to feel—and do—a hundred things that have never happened to me before."

The pad of his thumb traced her jawline. Maybe she didn't hear herself. But he did. Love—the kind that mattered—was terrifying and wonderful and totally unique to the two people who shared it. Nobody else had the same brand. Nothing was the same, once you'd taken the risk and crossed that certain line. "Ariel?"

"Hmm?"

"I have some land."

"Land?" The sudden switch in conversation didn't seem to bother her. In fact, she seemed relieved. Her fingers climbed the fuzzy hair on his chest and then looped easily around his neck. He had the brief suspicion, much as he loved her, that if he hadn't changed the subject, she just might have tried diverting him into talking about—or doing—anything else.

"Yeah, land. A tract of ten acres. Bought it years ago for a song, near Bridgewater. Lots of old farms around there, and it's a real quiet town, with clapboard houses and big overgrown maple trees and a village green. The tract was cheap, nothing on it but a falling-down old farmhouse and a couple of shacks. I had this idea about building a house, raising the kids there."

"But you never did?"

"No. In the beginning, I couldn't swing it financially—I needed to make a few years' dent on the land payments before tackling the expense of a house. Then came the divorce. Since the kids live with me, the cost of the divorce was never that rough, but then the problem was time. Between money and the lack of free time, I can't really explain why I didn't put that land back on the market and get rid of it—except I liked the idea of having a place where I could start over fresh. It has nothing to do with Nancy. It has nothing to do with anyone else. I love you, Ariel."

With a little luck, he might have slipped in that last comment without her noticing. He should have known better. She went all still. Her fingertips turned ice cold on the curve of his neck. She swallowed hard. "Josh—"

His heart lunged painfully. He knew her lack of faith in the institution of marriage. And he'd always understood that he was the worst of possible risks for Ariel—not just because the kids came with him in a package deal, but because a divorce labeled him a proven failure in the happily-ever-after department. Yet she'd stolen his heart in spite of the obstacles, and somehow he'd hoped that the time and intimacy they'd shared together might have dented her fears.

No tuna. A lump of dread lodged in his throat, too sharp and thick to swallow. From her face, from her stillness, from the leap of fear in her eyes, Josh had a clear measure of how wrong he'd been. To push her at all, he sensed, was to lose her—fast and for good.

"Hey, don't panic." He smoothed a strand of hair from her brow. "I don't know why I told you about the land. Just hadn't thought about it for a long time."

"It's a dream of yours."

"Yeah. And the middle of the night seems the only time it's easy to talk about dreams. And love. Still, there's love and there's *love,* Ms. Lindstrom. You've surely had men tell you they loved you before."

"Yes. I have, Josh. But—"

"It's a good word. A good feeling. Nothing that should be striking terror in your soul, green eyes."

Eleven

The word *love* had always struck terror in her soul.
Ariel understood perfectly well why the word fright-
ened her. People invariably got married because of
love, but that unpredictable ingredient never seemed
to save anyone from ending up in divorce court. It
hadn't saved her parents. It hadn't saved Josh.

The word was like a mosquito. She couldn't swat it
from her mind. Considering the deafening noise volume around her, she should have found it impossible
to concentrate on anything so serious.

Bruiser was down on the softball field, just picking
up a bat for his turn at the plate. Neither team pitcher
was going to win awards for skill—the score was 17-
17—but Josh's son was stuck with the pressure-cooker
responsibility of breaking the tie. It was the last game
of the season for the kids—the whiff of crisp breeze in
the air was a clear omen of September and that

dreaded word *school*. Parents packed the stands tighter than sardines, screaming support for their favorites and armchair-coaching at stereophonic volumes. Josh was one of the worst.

"Hey, Ariel, would you hold this?"

"Why sure, love bug." Ariel accepted the bag of popcorn from Killer. She knew little about softball, but it wasn't hard to figure out how these events worked. The dad's job was to scream, whistle and swear whenever his offspring did anything, good or bad. The mom's job—even an honorary mom—was to hold the popcorn, jackets, insect repellent, dolls, drinks, cameras and anything else the clan brought from home.

Nothing tricky about handling *those* kinds of mom's jobs. She was doing fine. Either by accident or intent, she'd had a number of chances to practice this honorary-mom business over the past couple of weeks. Josh had included her in a picnic with his clan, an afternoon horseback riding with the kids, and another time, a barbecue with a dauntingly uncountable number of Penoyers. Nothing had gone wrong so far, yet tonight her heart was uncontrollably filled with panic.

Next to her, Josh cupped his hands around his mouth to make a megaphone. "Ram that ball out of the park, Bruiser! Whack that sucker! You can do it!"

Ariel recognized a primal male in his glory. He shot her a wink, a grin, and squeezed her shoulders with a gorilla's pressure—then shot to his feet to yell more violent suggestions to his son. The drumroll of dread in her pulse increased.

Josh played the way he worked and lived and made love—100 percent investment, no-holds-barred. She knew he'd lied to her. He would never have used the word *love* lightly. Nothing he did was light, not in the emotions department, and from the start Ariel understood no affair would work for him—no relationship would work that wasn't leading toward marriage. His values were carved in marble. His kids were top priority and his life was chaotically busy. Only a lady in-house could make that kind of setup work...unless the lady was willing to settle for a few stolen hours on an occasional night.

He hadn't used her that way. He hadn't, in fact, shown up any of the nights in the past two weeks. There'd been no wild seduction scenes on her kitchen table, no more scaring her with how sneakily and powerfully he took her apart at the seams. Josh had carefully, deliberately, included her in his life—just not as a lover. She understood the blasted man perfectly well. He was playing for a home run.

Below on the ball field, in a more literal sense, so was Bruiser. His bat smacked the ball. A foul, she guessed, from the groans of the audience. The pitcher wound up and zinged another ball. When the ump called a second strike, Ariel surged to her feet, dribbling dolls and jackets and popcorn bags. What kind of damn fool jerk would call a strike when Bruiser hadn't even touched the thing!

"Uh, hon...the ball was straight over the plate. Bruiser didn't try to hit it. That's a strike."

"Who made *that* stupid rule?" Ariel muttered, but she couldn't sit down then. Everyone was standing; she couldn't see over the other heads and shoulders. Suddenly the whole crowd fell silent. The pitcher was hamming it up, turning his arm in circles—a freckle-nosed redhead that Ariel took an instant dislike to.

Josh filched a handful of popcorn. "You gonna survive this game?"

"I'm thinking about murdering that little pipsqueak pitcher. He's doing it on purpose. Making Bruiser wait, leaving him hanging..." She heard her own words, like the ricochet smack of a boomerang.

She knew she was leaving Josh hanging—participating in his life, inhaling the rich, sweet, dangerous feelings between them, but afraid to get off the fence. Unfortunately, the same things that worried her from the beginning had never disappeared. She wasn't a curtain fixer. She wasn't a housekeeper. And the insecurities she felt about taking on his kids, being any kind of good mom for them, refused to disappear just because she was crazy in love with their dad.

A hundred feet away, the pipsqueak pitcher finally let it rip...and Bruiser, *her* Bruiser, slammed that ball a zillion miles in the air and straight over the center field fence. Ariel cheered herself hoarse, and dropping everything, threw her arms around Josh for an exuberant whirl in the air. Oh, God, his eyes. So much love. So much intimate, private love in those dark eyes that, even in the middle of all that exuberant noise and celebration, she could see the guarded question still waiting for her.

His patience with her couldn't last forever.

It wasn't right to leave him hanging. Ariel knew damn well she'd run out of time for making up her mind about what she was going to do.

Josh seemed to be the only single dad participating in the first-day-of-school ritual. He gave his youngest one a last once-over. Patrice was dressed for success in all-new duds—tennies with fluorescent laces, floppy socks, skirt and a cute T-shirt, baseball hat. Her hair wasn't braided quite evenly, but God knew he'd tried.

"You already know half the kids," Josh told her.

"Yeah," she said mournfully.

"Everybody's a little nervous their first day, but you're gonna have so much fun you won't believe it. You'll be talking our ears off at dinner."

"Yeah," she echoed, even more mournfully.

"Now, I know you're scared—"

"I'm not scared, Dad."

"No?" She had a death grip on his hand. Thankfully the teacher spotted them in the doorway and promptly came over. He'd met Mrs. Betham before. She was a cute-as-a-button brunette, but to Josh, she looked no older than twelve.

"I'm so glad to see you, Patrice—"

"My name's Killer." Patrice immediately corrected her.

Without missing a beat, Mrs. Betham extended her hand. "Well, Killer, I've got a desk picked out just for you. Better give your dad a kiss pretty quick, sweetie, because I have all kinds of things to show you...."

His daughter didn't look too willing, but she transferred that death grip to Mrs. Betham. Over Killer's head, the teacher made a swift motion with her hand—informing him to scram. He understood it was time to get while the getting was good, but he still hesitated.

Ariel had offered to come with him this morning, but he couldn't see putting her through it. She didn't have a tough bone in her body, and was even a worse softy near his kids. Knowing Killer's feelings about school, he'd anticipated the squirt giving him a rough time. *Somebody* had to be tough, and he was pretty sure Ariel'd never manage it... but who'd guess he wouldn't, either.

His boys had had their first days of school, but somehow this was different. Killer was a girl. And his baby. The world was a big dangerous place for a baby, and he felt this clutching guilt in his chest, as if he were throwing her to the wolves.

He swallowed hard. Mrs. Betham hadn't made her take off the baseball cap. She also hadn't forced the issue of using Patrice's name, when his daughter really liked the rough-and-tough image of being called Killer. The child-faced teacher had shown some brains so far—surely Patrice would be okay for a few hours?

So he left.

Mrs. Betham connected with him via the cellular truck phone around one. Carpenters and plumbers were trying to work on the rush-build project at the same time his electrical crew was stringing wire. The noise level of screaming saws on the construction site was loud enough to wake the dead.

"She had lunch in the cafeteria, I know for sure. And she went out to play after that. There were two parents watching the kids on the playground, and they both saw her there. But when the bell rang for the kids to come back into school, she was gone."

"You lost my daughter?"

Possibly the teacher sensed that there were certain things no sane person would risk saying to Josh. Mrs. Betham's voice lost a whole octave. "We've checked the bathrooms, the cafeteria, the halls, the other classrooms—"

"You lost my daughter?"

"We had no reason to expect she was going to do anything like this, Mr. Penoyer. As far as I could tell, she had a wonderful morning. She's going to take to reading so fast, you won't believe it. The other kids got on with her fine—so I'm still not sure what could have happened. But we would appreciate it if you'd check to see if she's home—"

Josh had the truck started before even hanging up the phone. He'd check home. And then he was calling the cops, the National Guard, the U.S. Marines and the Mounties, preferably simultaneously. God knew, his youngest could outwit three out of four.

Ariel was just bagging a sale when the telephone rang. She waved goodbye to the customer at the same time she snatched the receiver. The caller never wasted a breath on a hello. "She's missing. I'm hoping like hell she's with you."

Josh didn't have to identify the missing party. Ariel already knew it was a red-letter day for his youngest, and had been thinking about the urchin all morning. "Josh, you *know* I would have called if she showed up here."

"Yeah, I know. But dammit, I'd really hoped—"

"Just take it easy. We'll find her. In fact, stay on the line for a second while I look around, okay? For sure, she isn't down here in the shop with us, but I'll run out back and look upstairs."

A half hour later, Ariel was upstairs in her apartment when she heard the thunder of footsteps. The whole clan burst through her door, which wasn't unexpected. Earlier, Josh had yanked the boys from school to do a neighborhood search, so they were with him. Killer's grade school and the police had already been called, so technically the crisis was over—everyone knew that Patrice was here, safe and sound.

Actually, she was sitting on the kitchen countertop, swinging her legs, holding a mug full of butter-brickle ice cream that had liberally transferred to her cheeks, and wearing a heart-shaped crystal pendant that bounced with every gesture she made.

"Hi, Dad."

Ariel couldn't take her eyes off Josh. He muttered a swear word that was most inappropriate for the childrens' tender ears, but his eyes lasered on his daughter, checking her over like he was examining priceless diamonds.

He said, "I'm gonna kill you," and then swooped her into his arms in a massive, sticky hug. "I'm *really* gonna kill you," he said again, but that sure as petunias wasn't how he was hugging her.

"You're pretty mad at me, huh?"

"I wasn't mad. I was scared. You *never* do that again, you hear me? If you're unhappy, you *call* me. I'll come get you. You never leave school, you never just wander around the streets where nobody knows where you are. And unless you want to be dead, Patrice, you'd better be listening to me."

"I'm listening. Boober's listening, too."

"I *mean* it."

"Okay, Dad."

He tipped her chin so he could see her face. She really was okay. His gaze dropped to the heart-shaped pendant around her neck. "What's this?"

"It's a tals'man. Ariel gave it to me."

"Ariel gave you a present for running away?"

"'Course not. You should have heard her yell at Boober!—whew!—and she was mad at me, too. But she gave me this for guts. This is the tals'man she wears when *she* needs guts. You wanna know how it works?''

"Yeah, I want to know."

"You hold on to it real tight when you're scared of something. That's it. That's all you gotta do. The only thing is—it would never work if you stole it from somebody else. They have to give it to you, free, like straight from their hearts. You can't ever really own something if you steal it, Dad. And besides that, stealing would break the magic."

"Magic, huh?"

"It may not work. You gotta test it. Because some tals'men have more powers than others. So, Ariel says I can wear it to school every day for a coupla weeks and just see, you know? Give it a chance. And if that doesn't work, we'll try another tals'man. She's got lots of them."

"I'm sure she does." For the first time since he walked in, Josh's eyes met hers.

Her palms suddenly dampened, slick with nerves. She'd never exactly planned giving Killer the talisman, because she *knew* how Josh felt about hokey things like magic. It was just...she'd had a very upset little girl on her doorstep, and she didn't have four hours to dither or think—Patrice was upset right *then*—and the urchin's fondness for magic seemed a natural way to reach her. If Josh had a problem with that...

But she couldn't tell what Josh was thinking. His gaze rested on her face, as snug-warm as a blanket that covered her head to toe. He made her feel...nervous, and he held that gaze for a long thoughtful moment before suddenly turning to his kids. "I think it's time we got out of Ariel's hair and headed home. She has a business to run. It's the middle of her workday."

The kids scrambled for the door. So did Josh, but once the clan bounded down the stairs out of sight, he paused in the doorway. "It's just like before, isn't it?" he mused. "You're worried. You're wringing those hands like there's no tomorrow. You thought I'd object about how you handled Killer."

"I know how you feel about magic, Josh—"

"No, honey, you don't." He shook his head, as if trying to clear a million mental cobwebs. "Damn. It's confounding, how totally I misjudged you. I thought you were a sane woman. I thought that no sane woman would want to take on my three hellions and a household of dirty towels. But you never gave a damn about the dirty towels, did you? And you've never once been less than crazy about my monsters."

"Towels? Who the patooties cares about towels?" The sudden twist in the conversation bewildered her. "And I don't understand what you're getting at—you surely know how I feel about your kids—"

"Yeah. I do. You've seen all of them at their worst. You've seen me at my worst, too. Nothing ever stopped you from caring about us—I'm not sure you even noticed you were in the middle of a tornado, sweet pea. All the things I thought were serious problems flew right past you. It's just the mom thing that scares you, isn't it—when damn, Ariel, I don't know how to convince you that you were *born* good at that. You give my kids love. You give them empathy and understanding. You give 'em magic. Your brand of magic. How the hell could you *not* realize how special that is?"

He shook a finger at her.

"I have to go. But you'd better believe it—we're not done with this, and if you're nervous now, I might as well warn you. When I come back, I'm going to give you some *real* reasons to shake in your boots."

Ariel had no choice about going back to work—Dot had both the afternoon and evening off—and the first of the month meant handling bills and extra book-keeping on top of handling customers. The phone rang a dozen times. Every time she jumped, even though it wasn't Josh. Every time the store bell tinkled, she jumped, too, and although the flood of customers was certainly welcomed, not one of them was Josh, either.

Ariel told herself she wasn't expecting him, not really, no matter what he said about coming back. He had kids to get settled and fed. And after a particularly chaotic day, the children had to come first with him. She always understood that. And anyway, she wasn't sure she wanted to see him…not while she was feeling this unsettled and edgy. She strongly suspected that he intended a showdown.

She wanted a showdown, too. The problem was that she had perilously huge expectations about how she wanted that shoot-out to go in their personal OK corral. Her whole life, she'd steered clear of expectations involving men and commitments. She would never have survived her childhood if she hadn't learned to be tough on herself—too tough to believe in hope, too practical to dream impossible dreams.

Like any ordinary night, she locked the doors at seven, flipped over the Closed sign, then methodically flicked off the lights. Once the money was scooped out of the cash register, she headed for the safe in the back room, and knelt down to spin the combination.

Handling money was the last job of the day, and normally her stomach would be grumbling and complaining by now. Oddly, she wasn't hungry for dinner. She wasn't even hungry for butter brickle. A frightening omen. Only the most monumental of catastrophes had ever put her off her butter brickle.

When she heard the rap on the back door, her hand flew straight for her stomach...then shifted to a more protective covering over her heart, which seemed to be beating louder than a stampeding herd of elephants.

Strangely, her heart immediately calmed down when Josh turned the knob and stepped inside. Positively there was no logic to her heart's behavior, because the view should have scared her to death.

"I told you I'd be back," he said. His tone came out belligerent, his voice as rough and tough as if a grizzled piece of rawhide was stuck in his throat.

"I know you did."

"The kids know where I am. They have express orders not to call unless the house is on fire. So for once, I think we can count on a conversation with no interruptions."

"I think we could use a conversation with no interruptions," she echoed. Quick as a blink, she bent down and yanked the workroom phone jack from the wall, then stood up straight.

"I want to get something straight first, though. I'm not here for my kids. Part of what I was trying to tell you this afternoon is that I understand—you've got fears about what kind of mom you'll make, and nothing that serious for you is going to disappear overnight. I *want* to talk to you about that. Just not now. God knows, I'd take a bullet for my kids, but this just plain has nothing to do with them. Make no mistake. I'm here for me.''

"I had that feeling," she murmured.

She'd never seen him in a suit before. The sight was riveting. The color was somber, serious navy blue, and the jacket made his shoulders look barn-broad. His hair was freshly washed and slicked back. The white shirt was dazzling bright next to his sun-bronzed skin, although the collar appeared to be choking him. So did the tie, which was truly a disastrous blue-and-yellow print.

She noticed the tie, she noticed that he shaped up dauntingly, deliciously well in a suit, and she especially noticed the dozen bloodred roses clutched in his hands. The roses were moving. Quivering, just a bit, as if they were sensitive to some faint breeze in the room, when of course, there was no wind anywhere around.

Possibly, Ariel thought, the reason she wasn't shaking in her boots was because her lover was so obviously shaking in his.

"I don't suppose you'd be willing to take these flowers off my hands," he said desperately.

"I sure would. They're beautiful, Josh." Unfortunately there was no vase in the back room, but there were certainly a zillion for sale out front. She whipped out in the darkness, came back with the first container big enough to hold water, and took care of those breathtakingly fragile roses at the speed of sound.

"I had something else I wanted to give you."

"Yeah?"

His hand dived in his suit pocket, then fumbled and groped as if the pocket were so huge, there were choices he had to weed through. His eyes, though, never left her face, his gaze as steadfast and tight as a magnet. "You gave that heart-shaped thing to Killer. I guess that's why I thought you might like this. It's a kind of talisman, too. At least . . . I hope you'll see it that way.

She opened the tiny velvet box. The ring was gold, with diamonds framed in a heart shape. The setting was delicate, but the light emanating from the stones shone strong and true, as eternal as fire, as enduring as magic. The real magic of love, she thought, and for a moment couldn't speak.

"It comes with a wedding band." His tone turned belligerent again, as if he were terrified to admit this. "I know damn well that other men could give you bigger diamonds. And I know, have always known, that I'm a helluva bad risk, with a failed marriage behind me and a crazy household that I just can't make disappear. But I love you."

"I love you, too," she whispered fiercely, but for a second, he seemed simply too distraught to hear her.

"You've brought magic in my life. Magic like I never believed in, like I never thought possible—not for me. I'm not a fairy-tale kind of guy, Ariel. You wouldn't be getting any prince."

"I never wanted a prince. I never believed in, or wanted, a fairy tale." She moved forward swiftly. He'd suffered long enough, she thought, with that dreadful tie and that strangling tight collar.

Her fingers were steady as she unloosened the noose of the tie. How ironic, to find herself feeling so steady and sure, when she'd been shakier than the San Andreas Fault on this subject for years. The difference—the only difference—between all those other years and now was the man standing in front of her. The guy with the shoulders as stiff as a lightning bolt. The guy with the wary, tense, scared eyes. "I *never* believed in marriage, Josh."

"I know—"

"I never *wanted* to be married." She hurled the tie.

"I know—"

"People build up these impossible dreams about marriage, develop fairy-tale expectations of each other. When that happens, it always fails." The button at his throat was tighter than a lock. She guessed he'd bought the new shirt, just for her. She undid those buttons, just for him. "I always knew that if I wandered down that yellow brick road, I'd fail at marriage no different than everyone else. I don't like divorce, Josh, and I damn well hate what divorces do to families and children."

"I know—"

"But I didn't know before. I didn't know I'd ever find a man as grounded in reality as I was. A man who knows what love is. Who shows it every time he's around his kids. Who sees past the mistakes people make, and the smoke-screen fears a woman throws in his way, and just keeps coming—"

"Um . . . Ariel?"

She checked his eyes. No wariness in them now, and barely a shadow of all that tense, masculine anxiety. Still, she wasn't through talking. "Pretty damn hard for a woman to be scared around you. She falls on her face—you're still there. She flubs big-time in front of your kids—you're still there. You just don't go away, not once you've decided to fight for something, Penoyer, and I know darn well you'd fight down and dirty to keep a promise. I never trusted anyone to be there. Damnation, you *forced* me to trust you."

She tried to help him out of his suit jacket, but he trapped her hands, tight, in his. "Lindstrom, could you put me out of my misery and just give me a yes?"

"I'm *trying* to tell you I love you."

"You did," he murmured, and then stole a kiss.

My Lord, she thought, he was an unprincipled rascal of a thief no different than his daughter. The emotion he poured into that kiss made her feel woozy and liquid-soft and soaring high all at once. Her heart fluttered wildly, then took wing. She never expected to find freedom with a man—the freedom within herself—to just let go. And test all the limits of what she could be as a woman.

She knew they had miles of trouble ahead. The advent of an inexperienced mom would require major adjustments from his whole household, and nothing, she guessed, would come easy. Once, that would have scared her witless, but that was before she had Josh in her corner. He wasn't going to run from trouble. He'd endured so many rough times that a promise from him had the weight of cement. He *loved* trouble—as witnessed by the lifetime of trouble he was certainly inviting at this moment.

He tore his mouth free from hers. For all of thirty seconds. "I didn't think you had any more magic tricks that I hadn't seen. But I should have known—you do. I would really like to think, love, that I had the self-control to take you upstairs before—"

"Pull the shade, Josh."

He pulled the shade. She used magic to obliterate the last of his self-control, all the magic of love she had in her. He understood all about the magic of reality, her Josh, and he certainly knew how to express love. There couldn't be a more natural way to start their lives together.

* * * * *

SILHOUETTE® Desire®

COMING NEXT MONTH

#937 THE DISOBEDIENT BRIDE—Joan Johnston
Children of Hawk's Way
July's *Man of the Month*, Zach Whitelaw, placed an ad for a responsible, compliant woman to become his wife. Unfortunately, the one woman who satisfied the fewest qualifications seemed most suitable for the job!

#938 FALCON'S LAIR—Sara Orwig
Ben Falcon was enchanted by the beautiful woman who couldn't remember her name. But once her memory returned, would he be able to forgive her true motive for appearing on his ranch?

#939 OPERATION MOMMY—Caroline Cross
Once they met Shay Spenser, single dad Alex Morrison's three boys decided she would make the perfect mom. So they launched "Operation Mom" and waited for the results!

#940 CAT'S CRADLE—Christine Rimmer
When Dillon McKenna found an abandoned baby in his truck, he immediately went to Cat Beaudine for help. But the sensuous woman he found definitely wasn't the tomboy he remembered....

#941 THE REBEL AND THE HERO—Helen R. Myers
Logan Powers didn't want anything to do with Merri Brown Powers or her son. But now he was forced to marry the one woman he had tried so hard to forget—his brother's wife....

#942 MIXED-UP MATRIMONY—Diana Mars
Tamara Hayward and Bronson Kensington had to somehow talk their kids out of eloping! Could they stop the wedding before Cupid's arrow struck these two sensible parents, as well?

Take 4 bestselling love stories FREE

Plus get a FREE surprise gift!

Special Limited-time Offer

Mail to Silhouette Reader Service™

3010 Walden Avenue
P.O. Box 1867
Buffalo, N.Y. 14269-1867

YES! Please send me 4 free Silhouette Desire® novels and my free surprise gift. Then send me 6 brand-new novels every month, which I will receive months before they appear in bookstores. Bill me at the low price of $2.44 each plus 25¢ delivery and applicable sales tax, if any.* That's the complete price and a savings of over 10% off the cover prices—quite a bargain! I understand that accepting the books and gift places me under no obligation ever to buy any books. I can always return a shipment and cancel at any time. Even if I never buy another book from Silhouette, the 4 free books and the surprise gift are mine to keep forever.

225 BPA ANRS

Name	(PLEASE PRINT)	
Address	Apt. No.	
City	State	Zip

This offer is limited to one order per household and not valid to present Silhouette Desire® subscribers. *Terms and prices are subject to change without notice.
Sales tax applicable in N.Y.

UDES-295   ©1990 Harlequin Enterprises Limited

You know where the MEN are....

SILHOUETTE®

Desire®

PRESENTS

Mr. January in
A NUISANCE
by *Lass Small*

Mr. February in
COWBOYS DON'T CRY
by *Anne McAllister*

Mr. March in
THAT BURKE MAN
The 75th Man of the Month!
by *Diana Palmer*

1995

Mr. April in
MR. EASY
by *Cait London*

Mr. May in
MYSTERIOUS MOUNTAIN MAN
by *Anne Broadrick*

Mr. June in
SINGLE DAD
by *Jennifer Greene*

And look for more sexy heroes coming your way in the second half of 1995!

MAN OF THE MONTH:
He knows what he wants...
and he knows how to get it!

MOM3-R

He's Too Hot To Handle...but she can take a little heat.

SILHOUETTE

This summer don't be left in the cold, join Silhouette for the hottest Summer Sizzlers collection. The perfect summer read, on the beach or while vacationing, Summer Sizzlers features sexy heroes who are "Too Hot To Handle." This collection of three new stories is written by bestselling authors Mary Lynn Baxter, Ann Major and Laura Parker.

Available this July wherever Silhouette books are sold.

SS95

Announcing
the New Pages & Privileges™ Program
from Harlequin® and Silhouette®

Get All This FREE
With Just One Proof-of-Purchase!

- **FREE Hotel Discounts** of up to 60% off at leading hotels in the U.S., Canada and Europe

- **FREE Travel Service** with the guaranteed lowest available airfares plus 5% cash back on every ticket

- **FREE $25 Travel Voucher** to use on any ticket on any airline booked through our Travel Service

- **FREE Petite Parfumerie** collection (a $50 Retail value)

- **FREE Insider Tips Letter** full of fascinating information and hot sneak previews of upcoming books

- **FREE Mystery Gift** (if you enroll before June 15/95)

And there are more great gifts and benefits to come!
Enroll today and become Privileged!

(see insert for details)

PROOF-OF-PURCHASE

Offer expires October 31, 1996

SD-PP2